W9-ADL-676

ليلىٰ

Leyla The BLACK TULIP

GIRLS *of* MANY LANDS

England ➳ 1592
Isabel: Taking Wing by Annie Dalton

France ➳ 1711
Cécile: Gates of Gold by Mary Casanova

Turkey ➳ 1720
Leyla: The Black Tulip by Alev Lytle Croutier

Ethiopia ➳ 1846
Saba: Under the Hyena's Foot by Jane Kurtz

China ➳ 1857
Spring Pearl: The Last Flower by Laurence Yep

Yup'ik Alaska ➳ 1890
Minuk: Ashes in the Pathway by Kirkpatrick Hill

Ireland ➳ 1937
Kathleen: The Celtic Knot by Siobhán Parkinson

India ➳ 1939
Neela: Victory Song by Chitra Banerjee Divakaruni

American Girl®

Published by Pleasant Company Publications

For information, address: Book Editor, Pleasant Company Publications, 8400 Fairway Place, P.O. Box 620998, Middleton, Wisconsin 53562.

Visit our Web site at **americangirl.com**

Printed in China.
03 04 05 06 07 08 09 C&C 10 9 8 7 6 5 4 3 2 1

PERMISSIONS & PICTURE CREDITS

The following individuals and organizations have generously given permission to reprint illustrations contained in "Then and Now": p. 181—© Christies Images/Corbis (Constantinople/İstanbul); pp. 182–183—Photo by Jake Rajs, NY (Hall of the Sultan); "Kraamkamer Ener Voorname Turkse Vrouw," J.B. Vanmour, Rijkmuseum, Amsterdam (harem women); Mary Evans Picture Library (slave market); pp. 184–185—© Musée d'art et d'histoire, Ville de Genève, "Femme franque vêtue à la turque et sa servante" de Jean-Etienne LIOTARD, inv. no. 1936-17 (woman and servant); © The Trustees of the National Museums of Scotland (shoes and caftan); Mary Evans Picture Library (veiled woman); pp. 186–187—Topkapı Sarayı Müzesi, 8/1067 (mosaic); © Stapleton Collection/Corbis (tulip); © Owen Franken/Corbis (Turkish girls today).

Illustration by Kazuhiko Sano
Illustration based on photo by Jake Rajs
Title Calligraphy by Linda P. Hancock
Photograph of Ms. Croutier by Jerry Bauer

Library of Congress Cataloging-in-Publication Data
Croutier, Alev Lytle, 1944–
Leyla : the black tulip / by Alev Lytle Croutier ;
illustration by Kazuhiko Sano.
p. cm. — (Girls of many lands) "American Girl."
Summary: While trying to help her financially destitute family, twelve-year-old Leyla ends up on a slave ship bound for İstanbul, then in the beautiful Topkapı Palace, where she discovers that life in the sheltered world of the palace harem follows its own rigid rules and rhythms and offers her unexpected opportunities during Turkey's brief Tulip Period of the early 1700s.
ISBN 1-58485-749-8 (pbk) — ISBN 1-58485-831-1 (hc)
[1. Slavery—Turkey—Fiction. 2. Harem—Fiction. 3. Tulips—Fiction. 4. Kings, queens, rulers, etc.—Fiction. 5. İstanbul (Turkey)—History—18th century—Fiction. 6. Turkey—History—Ahmed III, 1703–1730—Fiction.]
I. Sano, Kazuhiko, ill. II. Title. III. Series.
PZ7.C88525 Le 2003 [Fic]—dc21 2002155612

For Justine

Acknowledgments:
This book was a gift. It is the result of my editor Tamara England's fortuitous bus ride in New York City that led her to Talat Halman, an old friend I hadn't seen for years. I was enchanted by Girls of Many Lands from the very beginning, but I had to have the encouragement of my agent, Bonnie Nadell. Tamara became my editor and proved the magic of author-editor collaboration. Rebecca Bernstein gave me invaluable research assistance and Will Capellaro designed a beautiful book. Ilmi Yavuz and my Turkish publisher, Senay Haznedaroglu, sent me books about the Tulip Era. And as always, I'm grateful to Robert, who not only continued bringing me coffee and love notes, but who was the first to read the manuscript for me. To all, and to my readers, one thousand and one kisses.

Please note that some Turkish letters, such as the undotted *i* (ı), are used throughout this book. The undotted ı is pronounced somewhere between the *i* sound in the English word *big* and the *u* sound in *bug*.

Contents

1 *Georgia*

Ever since the disappearance of my father, our lives had changed drastically. My mother became desperate after we had sold nearly everything—even Father's most beautiful painting—distraught from not being able to feed her four children. She tried to convince us that my father would return someday. But I sensed that inside of herself, mother had finally given up hope of ever seeing him again. Slowly I found my myself giving up hope as well.

My father, Aslan, was a painter, the best-known artist in Georgia. We lived in a country of many Christian people, and he was famous for his paintings of icons. Practically every Orthodox church in Georgia contained one of his masterpieces—a face of a saint with a gold halo, an angel, or the Virgin

Mary in the fields. Father believed that God was something personal and private. It did not matter what religion you were.

"*Lailahi Illallah*," he'd explain to my brother and me. "There is no God but God. The important thing is to be a full human being. To manifest the gift given to you. To share it with the world."

It had seemed odd to me that he, a Muslim, painted icons, but I understand now that the most important thing for him was being an artist. That was his gift, the gift he passed on to my older brother, Cengiz, and me. We would gather around the fireplace to paint and practice calligraphy for hours. We also learned to read and write the *Mkhedruli* and the Arabic alphabets—Mkhedruli for the language of Georgia and Arabic for the Turkish language. Nothing gave me more pleasure than painting with Father—except maybe working in the garden with my mother. It was a double pleasure; we not only grew plants but we made paintings of them as well.

Father taught us about blending colors, glazing, and the subtlety of brush strokes. He taught us how to notice shadow and light and how to draw silhouettes. He also taught us to see beneath the surface of things.

But then came the wars, and our little corner of the world was squeezed between the two great forces of Russia and the *Ottoman* Empire, the kingdom of the Turkish people. Georgia's King Vakhtang created an army and asked Russia for military aid, but he was unsuccessful. Some said he later died of grief.

Although my father was not fit to be a soldier because of his slight physique and dreamy temperament, he, too, set off. He had been called by the Georgian army to go along as a war painter to record battle scenes. We all stood at the door and waved to him as he left with his paintbrushes and easel. He slowly disappeared toward the hills and became a dot in the distance. My mother rushed inside, and I stood there with Cengiz and the twins while she wept.

That image of my father disappearing has never left me—my father the size of a man small enough to fit into the palm of my hand. Sometimes I would take one of Cengiz's tin soldiers and hold it in my hand, pretending it was my father, and I would have imaginary conversations with him. He became my icon, with whom I shared all the secrets I kept inside.

That was the last we saw of Father. Although the war ended and we became part of the Ottoman Empire, and although the Georgians were free to return to their homes, he still did not come home. He was one of the missing. We said nothing to each other about it, but we all feared for the worst.

2 *The First Tulips*

After Father left, Mother and I enlarged our vegetable and flower garden with my brother's help. We grew every possible vegetable, enough for our family and enough to sell and trade. Mother had her hands full with my twin baby brothers, so Cengiz and I took the produce to the nearby village markets.

I also had a flower patch of my own. My favorite flowers were the tulips.

"You know what 'tulip' means?" Cengiz laughed. "It really means 'turban'—you know, one of those onion-like hats that the Ottomans wear."

"It's a good name for them," I said.

I'll never forget seeing my first tulips. It was the first spring after Father left. Cengiz and I had gone up to the hills to collect water from the mineral springs.

On the way, we got lost and found ourselves in a meadow that was splattered with purple flowers. At first we thought that they were irises, the earliest wildflowers of the spring. But as we got closer, we realized that these were uniquc. They were so beautiful in the slender way they formed an urn, then flashed their pointed petals toward the sky. Something inside us told us they were not to be picked—not yet, anyway. But we returned often to watch them grow that first season, to see them at different stages. It became our habit to detour to the meadow whenever we went to collect water. We discovered that the flowers didn't last long. Then, after they dropped all their petals and their stems and leaves faded, we dug in the earth to find their seeds.

"Look, it's growing out of an onion!" Cengiz said.

"You think it's edible?" I asked.

"Maybe."

"I dare you." I knew Cengiz couldn't resist a dare.

This time he surprised me. "You go first," he said. "Go ahead!"

I cleaned off the whiskers that had rooted around

the onion-like bulb and took a bite. I spat it right out. "It's bitter! It tastes awful."

"Maybe you have to cook it first." Cengiz laughed at my sour expression.

"Maybe it's not meant to be eaten. Maybe the tulips are just meant to be beautiful," I said.

We both remained silent, as if our minds had wandered off somewhere else.

"Cengiz, do you think Father is coming back?" I asked.

He hesitated before responding. "I don't know."

"But do you *think* he is?" I pressed him, wishing he would tell me what I longed to hear.

He shook his head and confirmed that we both feared the same unspeakable thing.

"What are we going to do? Mother says there won't be enough food or money to last through the year." We were already stretched. But we were also proud—too proud to show others how much we were in need.

"I'll join the army. I'm the only man in the family."

"Don't be silly. You're just a boy." He looked hurt, so I said, "How could you leave us all alone, Cengiz? Look what happened to Father when he went with the army. He disappeared, and now we have nothing. I don't want to lose you as well. Neither does Mother."

"We have to find you a husband, then—an old man with a lot of money."

I wanted to pinch his cheek, but he jumped up and dodged away, laughing. He'd spoken in a joking tone, but I knew he meant it. I chased after him as he ran and I threw the partly eaten tulip bulb at him. But he was so quick that he turned and caught it in his hand.

He stopped. "What would happen if you planted these bulbs? You have the magic touch. You can get *anything* to grow."

"Maybe you're right. It won't hurt to try," I said.

Together we dug up as many bulbs as we could carry home. There, I planted them all in my patch. I returned to the meadow as often as I could to dig more bulbs to take back. Cengiz helped me. We planted lots and lots of bulbs and prayed they would produce flowers the next spring.

We never again spoke of our father.

3 *Growing Tulips*

That winter everything froze so hard that we went ice-skating on the lake. We rolled deep in the snow and had snowball contests. Sometimes all this made us forget our woes.

But it was rough. We ate dried chestnuts and baked with chestnut flour. We were running out of firewood and there were so many cold days that we often dressed in layers and layers of clothes and hats. Some days we wore all our clothes, and huddled together at night to keep warm.

My mother was not doing very well. She looked gaunt, and there were dark circles under her eyes. The twins were growing bigger and were hungry all the time. So was I, but I tried not to complain.

Somehow we made it through the winter—barely,

and with only a little help from our neighbors. The first signs of spring—warm winds and green shoots coming up through the muddy fields—filled us with new hope.

When spring arrived, dainty leaves pierced the sun-warmed earth of the garden. Within a few days, a torch-like stalk within each cluster of tulip leaves reached to the sky. Then petals formed into a spear shape and slowly opened, unfolding one by one. Cengiz and I were filled with joy. We had succeeded! As each flower opened, we were surprised to see that not all were the same purplish tulips we had originally discovered and planted, but that they were in all colors of the rainbow. The bright patch of tulips made even Mother smile for a moment.

"Your father loved seeing the fields of tulips whenever he went up to the mineral springs. Before you children were born, I sometimes went with him," she said, looking sad again.

I wondered what made the tulips change color when transplanted. Some of them had burst into bloom with petals that looked like the feathers of a bird.

My heart filled with happiness to see such miracles, especially after that long, dark winter. I began making charcoal sketches and watercolor paintings of the tulips. Father's words echoed in my head. "Manifest the gift that is given to you."

The news of our flowers spread quickly. Soon, neighbors and other villagers came to see them. Among them was old Ilia, a scribe who had lived a long time and had traveled to distant lands. He knew many unusual things.

"These flowers are called 'lâle,' he said. "Did you know that the first tulips came from around here? Now they are cultivated in the north of Europe by the Dutch people. The Dutch got their first bulbs from one of the Turkish *padishahs* one hundred years ago. To commemorate this gift, every year since then they send a cart full of tulips back to the *sultan* in İstanbul—as interest for the tulips they received, you realize. But those Dutch, they went crazy with their tulips, and I have heard that their whole country went bankrupt. Rich people traded their large houses, businesses, ships, and farms for single bulbs. Imagine!

People even killed each other for them. It's odd, because now the Ottomans import bulbs from the Dutch."

Once he started talking, it was impossible to stop old Ilia. But I was interested in what he had to say.

"In İstanbul, the Ottoman capital, people breed and cross the bulbs and sell them for unthinkable prices. For example, one variety brought two wagon loads of wheat, four loads of rye, four fat oxen, twelve fat sheep, four barrels of *rakı*, two barrels of butter, one thousand pounds of feta cheese, a marriage bed with linens, and a sizable wagon to haul it all away. All this for just one tulip!"

This information confirmed my growing respect for the value of tulips, a value that went beyond just their beauty. "What do the tulips grown in İstanbul look like?" I asked him.

"They come in all shapes, and all colors except black," he told us. "Many have tried but no one has been able to grow a black tulip."

Then he examined my tulips. "You have not done so badly yourself, young maiden. I think maybe you have the tulip touch."

"My brother helped me," I told him.

I sensed that some of our neighbors were jealous because they had not been the ones to think of gathering and cultivating the wild tulips. Now that they had seen it done and realized that the flowers were something of value, they too climbed up into the hills and began stripping them of the magic bulbs.

Cengiz and I were filled with a great desire to grow unusual tulips. We cross-pollinated them. We even tried grafting some, especially the dark ones, trying to make them even darker.

But the roof of our house still leaked and we didn't have decent shoes. And because of the excessive winds and rain, the vegetable patch was not doing very well. The soil was too wet and heavy to welcome the precious seeds and produce the plants that would feed us and provide our livelihood. My mother looked so unhappy that I longed for a brilliant idea to console her, something that would ease her burden.

4 *The Strangers*

As summer ebbed, the autumn rains came—and the season for wild mushrooms.

Mother always said that mushrooms were from another star. Searching for them was like hunting for a treasure. They had a way of hiding, but once you noticed one, others began to show themselves. I loved the thrill of the mushroom hunt—stalking and finding, then carefully pulling them out of the sweet-smelling earth.

One crisp fall day, Cengiz and I went into the forest with the other village children to collect mushrooms, just as we did every year. There was going to be an auction in the square that evening, and the largest mushroom would earn a prize. I prayed it would be mine!

For a long time, we searched the forest without finding any signs, but I didn't mind. I liked being close to the earth, inhaling its rich smells of growth and decay. I was happy to be distracted from Mother's unhappiness, too. In better times, she would have been there with us. Cengiz and I ventured deeper into the forest, looking for pine trees surrounded by blankets of needles under which the *Boletus edilis*, delicious mushrooms with fat round stems, liked to nest.

I saw a promising dome-shaped swelling on the carpet of pine and gently pushed aside the needles with my hand to see if a mushroom was hiding. Sure enough, there it was, beautiful with a taut mahogany surface and spongy white undercap. It was enormous, even larger than my face. I knew the moment

I carefully twisted its stem and felt its weight in my hand that this had to be the prize-winning mushroom.

That evening the people of our town made a bonfire in the village square to celebrate the mushroom harvest. Families brought mushroom soup, mushroom tarts, and mushroom wine. Some of the children were even dressed up like mushrooms, wearing brown sacks with funny hats. Many species of mushrooms were displayed—the edible ones as well as the poisonous ones we all knew to avoid. Some mushrooms could be deadly.

"She has such a special touch with plants," I overheard old Ilia tell someone. "It's no surprise she won the prize this year."

"Yes, but too bad about her father. The poor family is having a very difficult time, I've heard. They should just find a good husband for her."

I slipped away, disturbed by this conversation about me. I had noticed some strange men in among the villagers and wanted to observe them more closely. They stood out as foreigners, dressed in fancy Ottoman clothes with white turbans and shining *scimitars*. People whispered that they were from İstanbul, the enchanted Ottoman city.

There were three of them. Two looked like brothers. Both were short and stubby, and one had a harelip. The third man was very tall and had a blond mustache. Their eyes swept the crowd as if in search of prey. The tall man's gaze came to me and fixed itself. Then, with his eyes still on me, he leaned down and whispered something to the other two men, who turned in my direction. I looked away, filled with a fear I couldn't name, and quickly disappeared into the crowd.

I fled home and gave my mother the round of cheese I had won with my mushroom. It was not much, but it would help.

As I worked in my garden the next day, I heard voices along the path and saw four men walking toward our home. The three of them were obvious with their turbans. The fourth was our mayor. I felt some danger without knowing why, and I slipped into the house. I ran upstairs to hide as my mother opened the door to let the men in.

I listened, my ear close to the floor, as the mayor translated to my mother, who did not speak Turkish. From what he said, it was obvious that the mayor was acting as an agent for these men, and they were talking about me.

"They'll take her to a good household in İstanbul and find her a husband of means. They are offering a very good price—surely enough to feed the rest of your family for a long time. I know how difficult it's been for you since Aslan disappeared. You'd no longer have to worry about supporting your daughter; she'd be out of your hands and well taken care of. Someday, she'd become a lady."

But my mother refused. "She's my daughter. She's still a child. I can't part with her."

"She is not a child anymore!" the mayor raised his voice in an impatient tone. "As I said, this is a good offer and you should think about it carefully. Think about your other children, too. Think!"

"No," my mother said. "I can't let her go."

The mayor's voice became heavy. "Very well. But keep in mind that these gentlemen will be here for another day only—in case you change your mind. You know where to find me."

The door slammed shut.

I knew that my mother was in a difficult position. She needed money so she could feed the family, and these men were offering money—but for me, her only daughter. I wished there was something I could do. I wished my father would come back. I wished we could all sit together around the fire, painting and studying like we used to, Mother strumming the *ud* in the background and the twins playing with the kittens. I wished our family could return to the days before the war.

The twins started crying and I ran downstairs to take them from my mother. Her face was stained with tears.

"I won't do it. I won't!" she said fiercely when she saw me.

I carried my brothers outside to the vegetable patch to dig some turnips and potatoes for our evening meal. The sun was beginning to set, and there was a hazy mist in the air that turned the evening to gold. As I paused to take in the magic of that twilight moment, an idea came to me, a way to help my family. But it was too frightening to even imagine, so I immediately pushed it from my mind.

"We'll figure out something," I told the twins. "Won't we? Now here, each of you can carry one of these beautiful turnips into the house so we can make dinner. Mama will be so pleased!"

The boys started jabbering in their private baby talk. As always, I couldn't understand them, but since they held out their hands and smiled, I knew they understood me.

5 *The Daring Choice*

That night, the men's faces kept returning to me in my dreams. I tossed and turned but remained between sleep and wakefulness. When I got up to drink some water, I noticed the tin soldier lying on the kitchen shelf. I held it in my palm with tears unexpectedly streaming down my cheeks.

"What do you think I should do?" I whispered to the soldier. As I looked at it, an answer came.

Follow your destiny.

Follow my destiny! But what did it mean?

By morning, I had made up my mind. I had a large mug of beet soup to give me strength, and I left the house as the sun came up.

On my way to the market to sell some garlic and potatoes, I passed by the *caravansarai* where I had heard the three strangers were lodging. Their camels were resting in the courtyard, slowly gnawing dried grasses gathered from our hills. Off to one side, the three Ottoman men were huddled around a low table, sipping tea and eating.

When I entered the courtyard, they turned around. I set down the basket of potatoes I was carrying and took a deep breath.

"What is it you want?" asked one of them in Turkish.

"Sir, is it true that you are looking for girls to take to İstanbul?" I responded, also in Turkish. I sounded a lot bolder than I really felt inside. My heart felt like it was jumping out of my chest.

The men seemed astonished by my question but, I think, even more by my brash behavior. "Why do you ask?" the tall one questioned.

"I know of a girl who might be interested," I said.

They looked at each other and then the tall one shrugged his shoulders. "It depends on the girl. She's got to be very special—pretty, talented, well-behaved." He watched me closely as he spoke.

"Well, how much, for example, for a girl . . . a girl

who is similar to me?"

They looked at each other again and the tall one asked the others, "How much is she really worth?" They all laughed.

"At least enough gold to take care of her family for a long long time," I said bluntly.

"This one's got spunk," the man with the harelip chuckled, looking at me. "Already bargaining before she has the deal."

"What she lacks is tact and poise," said his plump brother, with scorn in his voice.

That was a stab in my heart. I knew that I slumped forward when I walked. Mother was always telling me to stand up straight—at least she used to before Father left. My feet were too big for my size. And then there was the issue of my eyes, too large and widely spaced, a deep brown like my father's. Most people here had light-colored eyes.

"Early, at dawn tomorrow," the tall one said. "Tell your friend to be here at sunrise if she wants to see the world." He pulled out a pouch, took three gold coins out of it, and held them out to me. "And this is for the girl's family. Make sure it reaches them."

I reached for the coins.

"We don't normally do this," he said as he snatched his hand away. "How do we know we can trust you?" The brothers laughed.

"Because I will make a promise. And I always do what I say," I told them with unexpected determination.

"You'd better, or else there will be big trouble, not only for you, but for the girl's whole family . . ." growled one of the brothers.

"Don't worry. I'll tell my friend to be on time. She'll be here."

"And you make sure the girl's family gets the gold."

"Yes, I will," I said, nodding.

"Good. We'll expect you here. Tomorrow, just before dawn then." The tall man grinned as he flipped the three coins at me, one by one. Obviously he knew it was not a friend, but I.

I caught the coins in midair and felt their weight in my hand. "I promise," I said, then turned and hurried off to the market.

I was awake all night again. I tossed and turned. Finally, I couldn't stand it any longer, so I got up and quietly tiptoed outside. The sky was clear, and there were shooting stars everywhere. The air was crisp and fresh. I could sense the puttering of the night creatures all around me: A spider weaving a web. Owls calling in the forest. The moon illuminating the night landscape. It was such a perfect night. And I was about to say good-bye to all of it—to my home.

I visited my flower beds for the last time. Everything I'd planted with my own hands, the roses, the violets, the hyacinths, and, yes, my tulips. They were especially precious to me because I had brought them from the wild. It was as though I had tamed them. They had long ago dropped their petals, and all that remained now were their stalks with yellow crowns. I quickly dug up a few and separated their bulbs, which I carefully wrapped in an old shawl. These were the bulbs Cengiz and I were experimenting with. Now, some of them would accompany me on my journey.

I packed a few other things in a bundle—clothes, some paintbrushes, some of Mother's herbal remedies, and the little tin soldier. I wrote a letter to my mother and Cengiz telling them not to worry, that I had made a good choice. I told them how much I loved them and asked them to please forgive me.

Just before dawn, I went to my mother's bed and lightly kissed her forehead, then placed the golden coins under her bolster. She stirred in her sleep but did not awaken. On the other side of the bed, one of the twins giggled in his sleep. I saw that Cengiz had fallen asleep with all his clothes on, as usual. I covered him with his blanket and stroked his curly hair.

"Take good care of them," I whispered.

My cheeks wet with tears, I closed the door quietly, and left.

6 *Voyage to İstanbul*

Our voyage took us through the Caucasus Mountains. There were no other girls from my village, but we stopped at other villages along the way and picked up other girls who, like me, were destined for husbands in İstanbul. At first, we were too shy to speak to one another, but I thought from the looks we shared that we were all aware of what each of us might have given up to be on this journey. In the beginning, we traveled on camels. I'd never ridden on a camel before, and I was surprised by how fluid and graceful those huge animals were. Sitting up so high gave me a new perspective on my beautiful homeland. Later we rode in mule carts, our faces and bodies completely covered to keep out the dust carried by the winds.

After days of dusty travel, the air suddenly felt and

smelled different. We started seeing oddly shaped trees and flowers that I'd never seen before. One of the other girls said that it was the scent of the sea and that those were palm, lemon, and orange trees. We approached the largest city I'd ever seen, in the center of which were sparkling fountains.

"This must be İstanbul!" I cried, with a sense of thrill. "I thought it was much farther away."

"We have a long way to go before we reach İstanbul," the brother with the harelip explained. "This is only the city of Batum." He turned to Cafer Efendi, which I'd learned was the name of the tall man with the mustache. "Did you hear that? She thinks this is İstanbul." He laughed mockingly. "İstanbul!"

Cafer Efendi said nothing in return. I had noticed that he spoke less than the two brothers but with much more authority when he did speak.

I turned my attention from the men to where we were. Built along a vast, dark piece of water that had white screens floating in it, Batum was different from the mountains and valleys where I had lived all my life.

"What is this lake? It's so vast," I asked Cafer Efendi.

"It's the Black Sea, of course," he said tersely.

Father had often talked of the Black Sea and the White Sea, both of which he had seen as a young man. And here I was seeing it for real. For a moment, I forgot the circumstances that had brought me here, and even about missing my family. Instead, I felt excitement as I looked at the great body of water. The sea was indeed black and murky. Sailors often lost their way on the Black Sea, Father had told us. He had heard that it was famous for its treacherousness and was said to be inhabited by mermaids that caused shipwrecks.

"And those giant barrels floating in it with the flapping sheets—what are they?" I asked, pointing.

"They're not barrels. They are ships. One of those will transport you to İstanbul, if you make it that far . . ." he said casually.

"What . . . what do you mean?"

"You will reach İstanbul only if you behave along the way. Otherwise, you'll be thrown overboard, and you shall never see the magnificent *minarets* and grand palaces of the Padishah—our Sultan."

"What are minarets?" I asked, more curious than

worried by this threat. I had learned that he was not quite as harsh as he had first appeared to be.

"They are the thin towers on the mosques, the tall spires that pierce the sky, out of which prayers rise." He suddenly stopped himself. "You ask too many questions, girl," he said brusquely. "You'll have to learn to keep quiet. Otherwise, you'll get into trouble. I'm warning you."

Then he turned and strode away.

Later that day, we sailed out of the harbor on one of those ships.

At Batum, we had been joined by even more girls—mostly from Circassia and Abkhazia—who were also herded into the ship. The oldest girls were sixteen or seventeen, but some could not have been any older than three or four years old. All of them were very beautiful, even the little ones. All together, there were about two hundred of us who boarded the ship *Hürriyet*—which meant *Freedom*. It seemed a curious name for a ship carrying girls away from their families to a distant land to be married to husbands who were strangers. I whispered as much to another girl, who hushed me with a look at the brothers who were pushing the last girls on board.

"I don't think—" she started to say, but stopped when Cafer Efendi turned to glare at us.

My initial excitement at the idea of riding on the water soon turned to dread. Although our traveling thus far had been exhausting and sometimes hard, and some of the girls had cried themselves to sleep every night, it was nothing compared to what we now experienced. The ship was a floating dungeon. We were confined in a storage room so small that we had to huddle against each other. It was almost impossible to lie down to sleep. The floors were covered with hay, which soon started to smell. There were no windows or portholes, so we were in total darkness. The only time we saw light was when one of the men opened the door to hand in bread and water.

The voyage seemed like one endless night. The sea was rough, and I was seasick most of the time. Maybe that was fortunate, because it made me lose track of time. In the crowded darkness, breathing stale air, some of the girls fainted. At first many of the girls cried, while others screamed. The little girls called for their mothers. But when the noise level grew too great from the moaning and wailing, one of the men came in with a whip. There were more screams, then silence. I, too, was silent, lost in my memories and in a vertigo I could not have imagined.

At some point, Cafer Efendi appeared at the open door and called for me. I looked around in the dim light of the room, wondering what he might want with me. It was hard to move after being cramped up, and I must have taken too long to get to the door, because he impatiently reached in and pulled me to my feet, telling me to follow him. Unsteady from seasickness, I stumbled out onto the deck. Night was falling. The air and the wind felt so refreshing on my skin—a sensation I had begun to forget. I breathed deeply that fresh air, relieved to be outside. I searched the evening sky for familiar stars.

Cafer Efendi led me into a cabin where the brothers

and some other men sat on divans on the floor. The men raised their heads and scrutinized me. Cafer Efendi told me to hold out my hands and to turn them so these men could see them.

"This one has small delicate hands. They are lovely, but I doubt they could do much hard work even though they are a bit rough," Cafer Efendi said.

One of the other men spoke out. "Maybe she could play a musical instrument?"

"Possibly," Cafer Efendi said. He wrote something on a piece of paper, then turned to me. "How old are you, girl?"

"I am twelve."

He wrote that down, too.

One of the others reached out and lifted my eyelids. "Her pupils are fine, healthy looking." Then he forced my mouth open. "Her teeth are not bad either. Straight and white."

I could not stand them treating me like an animal at market, so I bit his hand as hard as I could. He pulled it away and slapped me. The others just laughed, as though what had happened was funny.

"No food for two days!" the man roared at me. "Now get her out of here," he said to Cafer Efendi, who grabbed my arm roughly.

I followed him back to the hold. "I told you to behave yourself," he growled. "Must we throw you overboard?"

He pushed me back into the hold and took another girl. The door shut behind them, and I was in the dark once more. As I tried to find a new spot, I tripped over someone. It was one of the little girls. I realized that I had hurt her and that she was sobbing dryly, trying not to make noise. I reached out and took her in my arms, and her sobs gradually subsided. She finally quieted down and fell asleep. I hugged her close, my face swollen from the slap I'd just received, and ached with longing for my twin brothers.

This is how my bond started with five-year-old Lena. Lena and I found comfort in each other. Taking care of her kept my own spirit alive. We talked softly and sang songs together. When the door opened and light spilled in, I could see her face and hair. She had long wavy white hair and looked like an angel. How could they give this baby in marriage to someone? I couldn't understand it, and I said something about it to the girls next to me. That's when one of the older girls shattered my illusions.

"What marriage? Don't you know they are not taking us to husbands?" she said scornfully, as if she thought I was slow. "We are *slaves*. They will sell us at slave markets."

This caused a great commotion among all the girls. They all started talking at once, in several languages. Those who could speak more than one language translated for the others. Some started to cry again.

"Shh!" warned the older girl. "Do you want them to come back in with the whips?"

Slaves! At first, I could not believe it. Then I knew she had to be right. How could I not have guessed from the way we had been treated? If we were going to be brides, they would have taken better care of us, pampered us in some way so that we would look well when we arrived. But wouldn't that also be true of slaves?

I closed my eyes and turned to my fate. I thought of

the words that had come to me when I held the tin soldier: *Follow your destiny*. Why had it led me to this? I would have been so much better off had I stayed with my family, even if we were so poor! Cengiz and I could have eventually found a way to support us. I missed him so much. I missed my mother and wondered if she had known that this was what would happen, if this was why she had refused to let the men take me. Now here I was on a ship called "freedom," a slave being taken to market. I had made a terrible mistake, and my only comfort was in knowing that my family did not have to worry about money for a while.

Finally the ship docked and the door opened. We were all pulled out of the hold. "Hurry, hurry!" yelled the brothers. As I stumbled up to the deck, trying to hold on to Lena's hand, I was stopped in my tracks by the striking landscape, filled with towers, that lay before us.

"This must be İstanbul," I cried. "And those towers the minarets." And even if we were going to be sold as slaves, at least we were leaving this terrible ship.

Cafer Efendi shook his head. "Not at all. Those are

the great towers of Trabzon that you see. Haven't you heard of them?"

I hadn't. "When do we arrive in İstanbul then?" I asked him, disappointed. I was so tired of this journey.

"We still have a long trip ahead. But not everyone is going to İstanbul. Some of the girls are headed for İzmir, Salonica, and Cairo."

I had heard of İzmir from my father, but I didn't recognize the other two places. "What about me?"

"You will be taken to İstanbul."

"And little Lena?" She was holding my hand tightly, her blue eyes wide. I don't think she understood what was happening.

"I cannot promise anything," Cafer Efendi said coldly. "And its not your business to know."

"Please, sir . . ."

Suddenly he relented. "Yes, she is going to İstanbul, also."

I could have wept with relief, but all I said was, "Thank you for telling me."

In Trabzon, they separated us into batches of fifty slaves each and put us on smaller boats, headed to our respective ports. Together Lena and I climbed aboard one of the boats bound for İstanbul.

The new boat was smaller and more cramped than the first one—and even more poorly equipped. It could not have been much longer than twenty feet. Once again we were stuffed in the hold, where we suffered constantly from thirst and seasickness. Heavy winds made this voyage even longer and rougher. It was so bad that I almost began to wish that the winds—or the mermaids my father had talked about—would dash the ship on the rocks and end the nightmare.

7 *City of the World's Desire*

Then one day the seas calmed, the doors opened, and light spilled into the ship's hold. The brothers told us to come out. As on the first ship, we had been in the same supine position for so long that it was difficult to untangle ourselves. Some of the girls collapsed and had to be helped up.

The brothers pulled us to the deck, snapping and snarling at us to hurry. I dodged out of the way, pulling Lena with me. We made our way through the other girls and leaned against the ship's railing, trying to stay on our feet. I breathed in the fresh air deeply for a few minutes, then turned to lift Lena up so she could see over the side of the ship.

The evening light was beautiful, filtering through a light fog. And through the fog appeared the most spectacular landscape I could ever imagine. Surely, I was dreaming, or feverish from the journey and only imagining the exquisite beauty before me.

We glided through a strait lined on each side with marvelous mansions and forests. There were all kinds of other boats around us. The first sight of the grand city was as if out of one of those *Thousand and One Nights* stories Father had once entertained us with. A continuous wall surrounded the city. Tall narrow spires, which sprouted on all the hills, had to be the minarets that Cafer Efendi had told me about.

We had arrived in paradise! My eyes were happy. This had to be İstanbul—one of the oldest cities and the most beautiful city in the world, or so old Ilia had described. How enormous it appeared, so much bigger than Batum or even Trabzon.

We dropped anchor and left the ship with the ragged bundles and baskets that held our few possessions. My legs felt unsteady on land, but I held Lena's small hand tightly, keeping her close to me. Filthy and rumpled from our long journey, we climbed into covered oxen carts and were driven away. Lena curled up in my lap and quickly fell asleep. As the cart rolled along, we competed for the spaces where the drapes were not completely closed in order to catch a glimpse of İstanbul. It was as though we were so mesmerized by the gorgeous city that we forgot the horrible journey we had just made.

I listened intently to the sounds, so different from the ones at home. Loud horns and then a man's voice, singing, filled the evening air. I followed it to one of the minarets. Then, from someplace else, another voice continued the same song. It was the *müezzin* singing. "*Allahüakbar! Allahüakbar!*" Our lullaby.

Cafer Efendi took several of us to a large house, one that was larger than any house I had ever seen. Several older women from that house immediately led us to a women's *hamam*—a public bathhouse—where we were scrubbed and cleaned and our heads examined for lice. Some of the girls had their hair cut, and some were deloused. I begged them not to cut Lena's white wavy hair. I told the attendant that Lena was a special being. The woman pondered this a little, then let her go. We were given clean clothes to wear, and I helped

Lena into her simple cotton gown after I put on my own.

Afterward, we were led back to the huge house where we were joined by girls who had come from different places. Some were unusual-looking, with skin the color of coffee. These girls were brought from a continent called Africa, where almost everyone had darker skin.

We had a hearty lamb stew with eggplants that night and slept in a dormitory that was clean and warm. It was the first real meal we'd had in weeks, and the first clean beds. Everything smelled as clean as freshly scythed grass. I was so exhausted from the voyage that I immediately fell asleep.

They had separated the younger girls from the older girls after our meal, and I didn't know where Lena was. Lena had cried, and I was upset, but I felt that if I called attention to it, somehow they would deliberately continue to keep us apart.

The next morning we were led through a winding stairway to a large room. Soon a very tall woman with broad shoulders arrived. She was dressed in a yellow *feradje*, a mantle, that was lined with blue and had buttons to the waist. A thin embroidered *yashmak* surrounded her face and descended to cover her eyebrows. She also wore a translucent white scarf that covered her mouth and neck. Her rust-colored striped inner dress was decorated with fur, which showed from under the edges of her skirt. The sleeves of her dress were so long that they completely covered her hands except when she pulled them up. Every finger had a ring of a different color. She wore dangling emerald earrings and spiky gold bracelets from her wrists to her elbows that jingled when she moved her arms.

From her tortoiseshell head decoration, or *hotoz*, to her jewelry, to her yellow shoes, it was obvious that she was a rich woman. She sparkled. I had never seen anyone as flamboyant.

The woman removed her veil. She had a strong and beautiful face. But if I hadn't known she was a woman, I'd have suspected that she was a man because she was so tall and muscular. She looked at each of us and nodded in approval.

"My name is Madam Siranush," she introduced herself, speaking in Turkish. "Now, I know you are simple girls with no manners, girls from all over the Ottoman Empire and or from even farther away. Over the next few days, I will show each of you how to walk like a willow and how to speak politely. I will teach you how to use your eyes to express yourselves. You are pretty girls, and I will polish you." Madam Siranush sat down gracefully. "You must work hard, and you must obey," she said firmly.

We worked from morning till night, learning how to walk gracefully, how to sit down properly, how to serve guests, and how to speak sweetly in proper Turkish. I was glad that I already knew Turkish, and I felt sorry for those girls who did not know how to say anything. Within a few days we were no longer girls from the Caucasus or other far-flung parts of the Empire. We became girls from İstanbul—at least on the outside. Inside, well, we didn't dare speak of that.

There was a lot we didn't dare speak of, including what was to become of us. But I did manage to discover that all the little girls, including Lena, were being kept in another part of Madam Siranush's household. I hoped I would be able to catch a glimpse of Lena soon. And I hoped she wouldn't get into trouble because she was crying for me.

8 *The Poet's Gift*

After several days of this kind of training, Madam Siranush gathered us in her courtyard. She was dressed even more extravagantly than usual, complete with veils. She told us it was market day and customers would soon be arriving. "Treat them very nicely. Smile at them" were her instructions.

Customers came and went all day long as we stood in small groups. All the customers were men. In this new world, women and men seemed to always be kept apart.

I heard one of the customers tell Madam Siranush, "Give us a dozen of them. The *Pasha* wants more for his *harem*."

His words felt like a stab to my heart. They were treating us like merchandise, like eggs or chickens. "A dozen of them." And that's exactly what happened—

Madam Siranush very coolly counted off twelve girls, who accompanied the man outside. Just like that, they were gone.

Some other buyers bought several girls. All kinds of exchanges were made, and payments included anything from sacks of bulgur to gold coins. By the end of the day, Emine, who I had become friendly with, was exchanged for a suit of armor. Another girl was exchanged for a horse. Many girls were sold, but I was not among them. Maybe these customers could sense how much I despised them, and that was why they left me alone. I was both relieved and worried. What would become of me?

More customers arrived the following day. Still, not many of them were interested in me. I was beginning to feel restless. As I stood there, I became aware of a man in a costume that was embroidered with flowers in golden thread—a costume I would expect only a woman to wear. He was watching me. I noticed a depth in his eyes that did not look at all frightening.

He looked at my face and nodded. "Interesting," he muttered. Then he dipped into his pocket, pulled out a shiny coin, and tried to give it to me.

"It has the Padishah's *turah*. Go ahead and take it. You might need it someday. And I am repaying a debt."

"But who is the Padishah?" I asked him.

"Our Sultan Ahmet—the King of Kings, the Unique Arbiter of the World's Destinies, the Master of the Two Continents and the Two Seas, and the Sovereign of the East and the West."

"And this city is his kingdom?"

"Bu şehrı Stambul ki bimislü bahadır." He recited a poem and smiled. "My child, the Padishah's empire stretches all the way to Italy and the great Alps Mountains in the west, to Persia in the east, and it includes all of North Africa as far as Morocco. Our Padishah could conquer all of Asia and Europe, but

he is a peace-loving monarch. He wants to end war and slavery and bring enlightenment to the world."

I had no idea what he was talking about.

He sensed my confusion. "Of course, you have no notion where all these places are, nor have you ever seen a map. You have no idea how vast this world is. How many different creatures inhabit it. And how many different kinds of people live in it—people who harm each other unnecessarily. I support neither slavery nor war. Those misfortunes should be removed from our destiny. Neither does our Padishah and his *Grand Vizier*, İbrahim Pasha, support war and slavery. Life is too short and precious."

I was dumbfounded. I wanted to know what he was talking about. What was a map, for example? He had to be an intelligent man, because he said so many things I didn't understand.

He noticed my confused expression. "Poor girl, you'll never know what I'm talking about. You are merely a slave. Still, may *Allah* bestow a happy fate upon you. Take and keep this coin for yourself. It is freshly made, for the first time ever, in our own mint."

"I don't understand what you mean by 'mint,' sir."

He smiled. "It is a place where gold is made into money."

He put the coin into my hand. "This is the *Cedid Zer-I*, equal to the Venice gold coin. Don't let anyone take it away from you. It will bring you good luck. Put it in a safe place."

"Sir," I said, "thank you for your kindness, but I can't let you go away empty-handed. I have to return the kindness." I reached inside my sack, which was on the ground near the wall, and I pulled out one of the tulip bulbs and gave it to him.

He immediately recognized it. "It's a tulip bulb. Very precious. How do you happen to have it?"

"I grow tulips. Or rather, I used to grow them . . . before I was brought here."

"How graceful of you to share it with me, then. It gives me hope that maidens like you appreciate beauty. Thank you, young maiden. I'll plant it in my own garden and compose a poem for it. I cannot purchase you because my job is to seek inspiration, not slaves. You have inspired me and you deserve to be taken to the best of homes. I'll see what I can accomplish. Farewell for now."

I felt a ray of hope. This strange man who recited poetry had brightened my day. *It is amazing what happens when people are kind to each other*, I thought. Yes, I'd given him one of my most valuable possessions. But it was a small price to pay for what he had given me in a moment of kindness.

That night there was more room in the large room where we slept, since so many of the girls were already gone. I had heard Madam Siranush talking to a man. "If they don't sell the first day, the chances of selling later are very slim," she had said.

"What happens to the girls who are not sold?" he had asked.

"Oh, we have ways of using them. We can turn them into beggars and thieves, or . . ." she waved her hand. "You can be sure none goes to waste."

I knew what beggars were. I had seen them pass through our village and I didn't wish to live such a life. I was told that first they were crippled—their arms or legs were broken, or they were made blind in one eye.

I prayed to have someone—someone nice—take me. Anything would be better than being maimed and forced to beg.

I had been unfriendly and cold at the market, despising my potential buyers. I had been scornful of all, except for the poet who had not been looking for a slave. Tomorrow, I decided, I would act friendly and make them like me better. I'd do anything to avoid becoming a beggar or a thief, and this might be my last chance. At least that's what I thought.

I learned from one of the servants that all the little girls, including Lena, had been sold to one buyer, someone here in İstanbul. My heart ached with worry for Lena's destiny. I'd hoped against hope that somehow they might let us stay together. Knowing she was gone reminded me all over again of everything else I had recently lost.

9 *Master Hyacinth*

The following day, more customers arrived.

Suddenly there was a commotion, and an impressive-looking man dressed in a long robe and a sable coat—like the winter coats worn at home—arrived. He wore a large cone-shaped turban on his head, but unlike the rest of the men, he had no beard or mustache. His skin reminded me of the rich color of an eggplant and appeared as smooth as a woman's. He was shaped like a pear and he walked with a delayed sway, shuffling in pointed shoes, which made him look a little comical. I of course didn't know who he was, but from his clothing, the way he moved, and the way Madam Siranush acted, I could tell that he was someone important. Behind him walked two other such men.

Madam Siranush had lined us all up. The pear-shaped man walked around and studied every girl. He stood for a long time in front of each one, then walked all around her, looking up and down with a critical stare. My heart was skipping, afraid that he would do the same to me—and afraid that he wouldn't. They say that what you fear most is what will happen to you. And then there he was, facing me, scrutinizing me. Despite my resolution to be friendly and cheerful, it was difficult to pretend.

"What sad eyes. Come on, girl. Smile!" he ordered.

I was so startled that I froze. It was his voice that surprised me. It was so high-pitched and so much like a woman's. It didn't fit his powerful shape. How could this small voice be coming out of this big man?

"I have asked you to smile," he repeated, with a dramatic frown.

Still petrified, I stretched the corners of my mouth.

"That's not a real smile. I want you to smile as if you are happy. As if you are feeling good, having fun. Not only with your lips but with your eyes. From the inside. I want to see your life, your vitality. Your spirit.

Life is precious, my girl. Don't cry it away."

How could he expect me to look happy when I was nothing but a slave, so far from home and far away from everyone I loved? Happy, not knowing where I was going to end up? Happy, being sold at a market like a horse or a sheep? But when I thought of the special moment with the strange poet the day before and I forgot where I was for just a second, the memory made me really smile.

"There you go. Nice teeth," the man said. "But the smile is even lovelier."

His words reminded me once again of where I was, and involuntary tears rolled down my cheeks.

"You seem to know how to smile *and* how to weep. There's not much difference between the two. That's often a good omen." He turned to Madam Siranush. "We should discuss the terms, Madam."

Madam Siranush's eyes were sparkling with excitement. "Look at her! Her pearl teeth, her willowy walk, her eyes tinted with every color of the autumn. She is a gem. It's possible I won't let her go."

She had grabbed hold of my shoulders and was

turning me around to give him a better view. I was really surprised to hear her say those things about me. She had treated me all this time as if I were a scarecrow. But the minute someone had shown interest . . .

"That's up to me to decide." He threw a small sack onto the table for Madam Siranush.

She weighed it in her hands without counting. She laughed and pushed it away. "We are poor, but not that poor, Sümbül Ağa."

The man's name was Sümbül Ağa! How funny, I thought, since *sümbül* means "hyacinth." Master Hyacinth. Despite his strangeness, I took a liking to him. He doubled the amount. Madam Siranush rebuffed him again. They were obviously bargaining for me. I was not sure whether to be insulted or delighted. But I prayed that it would be Master Hyacinth and not Madam Siranush who would finally claim me, although I had no idea who this man was or where he would take me. He was mysterious.

Finally they settled on terms, and the exchange was made. Master Hyacinth told the two men accompanying him to take me away. I was now his. At least, so I thought. I grabbed my sack, and then they took me out of Madam Siranush's house and put me into a fancy carriage drawn by two handsome black horses. It was completely covered except for the lattices through which I could get a breath of air. The horses started up, and we moved swiftly away. Occasionally, through the lattices, I could make out the silhouettes of mosques and other structures.

As the carriage rattled on, my curiosity grew. Where were they taking me? Who were these odd men? Why did Master Hyacinth have such smooth skin? Why did he and his companions speak with girlish voices? What kind of world was I entering? What if it was worse than what I imagined? And Lena—now that I had been sold to Master Hyacinth, would I never have a chance to see Lena again?

I counted the beads of my *tesbih* and prayed to Allah, as I had done so often on this peculiar and frightening journey I was on. I prayed for kindness. I prayed for good luck.

10 *Beyond the Gate of Felicity*

The late autumn sun was weakening as we rolled through the city. In the dimness of the carriage, I dozed off, tired after three days in the market and so much uncertainty. When I recovered myself, the two men were letting me out of the carriage and leading me on foot through an enormous gate.

"Where are we?" I asked.

"We are entering the Gate of Felicity," said one of them as we passed through the gate.

"What does 'felicity' mean?" I asked.

He looked at me with an odd expression. "Curious creature, aren't you? We're at *Topkapı Palace*, of course. And 'felicity' means happiness—bringing happiness to others. That part of it is true. But you'll soon discover that once you've passed through this gate, there is no going back."

"There is no going back? Then what lies beyond the Gate of Felicity?"

He didn't answer the question but instead led me through a large ornate door. I followed him along a corridor that had inscriptions painted or carved on the walls, all in the most delicate calligraphy. Their style reminded me of my father's, but they were gilded and showed even a finer stroke.

A *kilim* runner that looked like those we had in Georgia led to yet another door. At the end of the corridor, the dark man who accompanied me stopped and turned me over to the custody of an old woman, who was waiting at the door. She looked like a skeleton, very tall and faded. I followed her, clutching my bundle and wondering who she was. And where exactly were we? This was like no other place I had ever been.

The old woman led me through labyrinthine corridors with gorgeous tiled floors and walls that were lined with stained glass windows. Crystal chandeliers hung everywhere. I had never seen such beauty. I wondered what Father would say about such splendor and craftsmanship. Then she led me up some marble stairs into an enormous hall constructed entirely of wood.

"This is the dormitory of the *acemis*," she explained.

"What are acemis?" I asked.

"That's what we call novices—the beginners—like you," she said. "The girls who are new. You will be assigned to one of the departments and begin an apprenticeship. You are an acemi until you master your training."

"How long does the training last?"

She smiled dryly. "That depends," she said, "on your talents."

I wondered what talents she meant.

She pointed at a cabinet that stretched along the wall. "I see you don't have much, but you may keep your things there. Your mattress is also kept there during the day. You pull it out at night and make your bed. In the morning, you put it back in the cabinet. But first we'll have to get you cleaned up. The hamam is ready, and many of the novices are already bathing." She paused and looked at me, as if noticing me for the first time. "What's your name, girl?"

"Laleena."

"Laleena? What a sweet name! Enjoy it while you can, Laleena, as it will soon no longer belong to you."

"Yes, ma'am," I said. I had no idea what the woman was talking about. What did she mean, my name would soon not belong to me? I'd had it since I was born. It was mine. How could a person lose her name?

She gave me a pair of very tall wooden clogs with mother-of-pearl inlay—like the pretty boxes we had at home—and led me down another series of corridors. How would I ever find my way in so many corridors? How could I ever be expected to walk in such tall shoes?

This hamam looked nothing like the public baths

that smelled of sulfur that we had gone to while at Madam Siranush's. This one was an immense domed space with high walls of large slabs of white marble, decorated with colorful tiles in geometric patterns. The last of the evening light came through the star-shaped windows above the hamam's dome and spilled everywhere, as if passing through a prism.

The whole place was filled with steam, and barely visible within it, girls of all ages and all colors of skin were bathing. There was a strong echo, and voices and laughter resonated all around. The girls were scrubbing each other's backs and washing one another's hair. They were all naked. I had never been naked in front of others before, even at the public hamam, and I did not want to take off my clothes in front of these strangers.

The bath attendant allowed me to keep my chemise on. "Most girls are shy like you when they first arrive. They get used to being natural little by little. We all have bodies. Bodies go through several changes in our lifetimes, and your body is changing now. You have nothing to be ashamed of. But if you feel more comfortable covering yourself, go ahead, that's fine with me. Leave your chemise on, if you like."

A group of girls turned in my direction and whispered something among themselves; then they all burst into giggles. They were no doubt making fun of me. I felt as though I were on stilts, walking awkwardly on those tall wooden clogs, terrified of slipping and falling. I was sure that I must look ridiculous and that they were laughing at me.

"Don't pay attention to them. Just go ahead and take your bath," the attendant said kindly to me, then turned and told them to mind their own business.

She left me there and went off to attend someone else. Left alone, I wasn't sure what to do. Was I supposed to wash myself in a special way? I sat by the low marble sink and watched out of the corner of my eye what the other girls were doing.

First they sat around sweating in the hot steamy room as the steam became denser and denser. Then thcy sat by the marble sinks and poured water on themselves and screamed. I reasoned that it had to be cold water to make them scream like that. They washed and scrubbed themselves with pumice stones.

Finally, an attendant came and rubbed them again, this time with something that looked like oatmeal. After that, they returned to the sinks and rinsed themselves again. They next went into a deep pool. I could hear them gasp and squeal, so I guessed that the pool also held cold water. The hollow echo of their voices and laughter carried through the steam.

I'd never seen anything like this, even though I had been bathed at the hamam with the other girls from Madam Siranush's. Those baths were much less complicated and not fancy at all, and I had been so tired from the journey that I had hardly paid attention to what was happening. But I knew that I needed to pay attention here, since this seemed to be my new home. I decided to imitate the other girls so they wouldn't laugh at me. I did not want to lose my dignity.

After the bath, the old woman returned and took me to a small closet of a room instead of the dormitory she had shown me earlier. She told me that I would sleep alone here and that I was "under quarantine" until I could be interviewed the following day. Interviewed by whom? I was curious, of course, but

I did not ask. I remembered how angry Cafer Efendi had become when I asked too many questions, and I did not want to start off with making anyone angry. I had learned that I would find out soon enough, anyway.

"Try to sleep well, if you can," the old woman said as she closed the door. "And remember your dreams. They say that your first night's dream at the palace is prophetic."

There were no windows in the small room, and it was pitch black. I lay awake, imagining invisible spirits and ghosts dancing around me. To distract myself, I turned my thoughts to my family and to little Lena. I wondered if my father had returned home. I wondered where Lena was, where they would take a child like her. I was scared—almost as scared as I had been on the slave ship, cramped up with all the girls. And yet, they kept telling me that this place was a palace. My thoughts continued to swirl as I recalled the beauty of the tiled corridors and of the baths, and the weight on my heart lifted slightly. In the midst of such beauty and artistry, could things be so bad? Finally, the soothing effects of the bath worked and I slowly relaxed, drifting into a night full of dreams.

I dreamed that my father was alive and that he had returned home. My mother was beside herself and fell into his arms, sobbing. The twins ran around, talking their secret twins language that no one else could understand. Cengiz had a mustache and his voice was becoming deep. Father looked so forlorn when he discovered that I was gone. Finally *he* was home, but now I was gone, having been sold into slavery. I was somewhere far away, but my family did not know where I was or what had become of me.

11 *Leyla*

In the morning a girl only slightly older than I came and asked me to follow her. She sneaked a shy peek at me as we walked and told me we were going to the infirmary, but I did not know what an infirmary was. We went down the stairs and into a room where other girls were waiting. There, a woman examined each of us to make sure that we did not have any diseases, defects, or imperfections. There was another inspection of my teeth, eyes, ears, hands, and feet. Until I left home, I had never been so thoroughly examined. But being examined by this woman was not as humiliating as it had been being examined by Cafer Efendi and the awful traders.

After the inspection, I was led out of the infirmary by the same girl. There were so many corridors, so many stairs! The palace was like a confusing maze. I tried to pay attention to where we went so I could learn my way around, but it was impossible to keep it straight. Occasionally we encountered other girls carrying laundry or trays of bread and flower arrangements.

A large door led us to some apartments that even I could guess had to belong to an important person. Another dark man opened the door.

Inside, a large woman sat on a divan, surrounded by beautiful carpets. The girl gently pushed me forward toward this imposing woman. She was smoking a large *nargileh*, a water pipe. Her hands and bare feet were decorated with elaborate henna designs, and she wore gold bracelets all the way up her arms that jingled every time she moved, even slightly.

"Come here," she said. "And turn around. Let me see."

I obeyed, feeling awkward and slightly resistant to yet another inspection.

"Let me see your hands," the woman said.

Why was it that they all wanted to see my hands? I knelt down in front of her and held out my hands, self-conscious because I'd been chewing my nails. My hands were rough from all the gardening and outdoor work I'd always done.

"Alas, they are too small," she told me. "Too small for housework. I hope you have some skills."

"Skills? What do you mean by 'skills'?"

"Like sewing, cooking, making sherbets, playing an instrument, healing, dancing . . . "

"No, I don't have any skills."

"I see that you speak Turkish, although they tell me this is not your first language. Can you also read and write?"

"Yes, I know the Arabic alphabet and can read and write Turkish as well as Georgian. I . . . I also paint." I told her briefly about the icons.

Her eyes opened wide. "You must never mention painting here! Especially painting the likenesses of human beings. That is God's work, girl—Allah's work. It's sacrilegious, and you must forget all about it." She paused for a minute and composed herself. She drew heavily on her water pipe. Then she looked back at me. "Nothing else? You have no useful *talents?*"

"I'm not sure what you mean, ma'am," I said, struggling to understand what she wanted.

"A *talent* is a gift that one possesses naturally, unlike a skill, which one learns to cultivate. A talent is Allah's gift."

"Well," I stuttered slightly, "I think . . . maybe . . . I have some talent for growing things, like plants and flowers."

"Flowers?" This seemed to pique her interest. "Oh yes, I was told something about this."

I didn't understand how she could possibly have known that about me. Who could have told her? I realized as I stood there that I shouldn't have mentioned the painting. I knew it was forbidden to imitate Allah's work—that's what the *Koran* said. But devout as he was, Father had always painted, even icons. To manifest the gift he was given, he always reminded us, was also doing Allah's work.

I turned my thoughts back to the conversation at hand. "I can grow hyacinths, lilies, carnations, tulips," I told the woman.

"Tulips! You say you can grow tulips?"

"Yes, ma'am."

"Well, growing tulips is a talent. It also takes a special skill. People spend a lifetime perfecting it, you know."

"Yes, ma'am."

"So, you're a tulipist," she said in a hoarse voice, laughing at this word. "And what is your name?"

"Laleena," I said.

"Laleena? Sounds like a gypsy fortune-teller's name. La-la-la. From now on you'll have a proper name—a Turkish name for a Turkish girl. You'll be called *Leyla*."

"Leyla? But—"

"There are no buts. We change everyone's name so they can forget their past and become new people. Along with the other girls who can also read, you will study in the *medrese*. You will have Koran lessons. You must also learn to move more gracefully, like a willow. You hunch forward too much now."

I corrected my posture and held my head up. I had my pride.

"You will also be instructed in speaking properly. You know, you speak with an awful accent now, like a cow chewing grass."

She clapped her hands, and the girl who had brought me here was at my side in an instant. I noticed how beautiful she was, plump and apple-cheeked, very fair with blue eyes and blond hair. "I assign her to the Mistress of the Flowers," said the woman with finality.

"Yes, ma'am," said the girl.

I realized that I was dismissed. I got up. I wasn't sure how I was supposed to take my leave. Then I saw the girl touching her head, lips, and heart, taking a bow. I tried imitating her.

The woman watched me critically. "Teach her how to make a proper salutation, and keep her fingernails clean. Her hands should be hennaed. And her feet also."

The girl bowed again, then started for the door. I followed her.

"What name did she give you?" the girl asked me excitedly as we stepped back into the corridor.

"Leyla," I said, trying it out for the first time.

"Leyla, that's a beautiful name! Not so different from your real name, which they told me was Laleena.

You're lucky," the girl said. "You know what 'Leyla' means? It means a dark night, a night full of stars. I wish I had a name like that."

"What's your name?" I asked her.

"Belkıs."

"That's a nice name, too. I like it." Belkıs was being friendly, which encouraged me to ask her another question.

"Who was that lady?" I asked quietly.

"The *Kahya*—the Chief Housekeeper. She assigns each new girl to a department for apprenticeship, based on her look, talent, or skills. She assigned you to the Mistress of the Flowers—as she did me. It's what I usually do, except today they told me to help with you. We care for the interior harem gardens."

"The harem gardens?"

"Yes, the gardens inside the harem are quite vast and varied. We have kitchen gardens, healing gardens, scented gardens, and beautiful flower beds. You'll see."

I felt a tinge of excitement. The fact that I'd be working in the gardens was a sign of good luck.

"If you do well as an acemi, you get promoted in no

time," Belkıs continued as we walked through more corridors. "If you don't do so well, sometimes they move you to a different department, like they did with me. When I first arrived, I was assigned to the *Haseki Sultana*."

"Who is the Haseki Sultana?"

"The Number One Wife of the Padishah. It was a nightmare. There are so many other women trying to plot against her and her son. We were always afraid and suspicious. It is not a good way to live one's life. I'm much happier in the gardens."

I was getting more and more confused. Padishah? The Number One Wife? Threats from other women? What kind of place was this that *kısmet*, my fate, had thrown me into?

"What if a girl doesn't get promoted?" I asked Belkıs.

"Then it's her bad luck. Or maybe someone has given her the evil eye. They may get rid of her."

The evil eye? I looked at the pendant around Belkıs's neck, the blue bead with a white center that resembled an eye. I knew this was to protect her from the evil eye, because I wore one, too, pinned to my shoulder. "Could you tell me something? Where are we? People have been calling this place the palace. What kind of palace? And whose palace?"

"Of course, you don't know anything yet. I didn't either when I arrived here. We are at Topkapı Palace. It's the home of our Padishah, Sultan Ahmet, the ruler of Turkey and the Ottoman Empire. It is the most splendid of all the palaces in the empire of the Ottomans. We are in the harem, where all the Sultan's women and children live. There are no other men allowed inside, except the Sultan's sons—and the *eunuchs*, of course, but they are not really men."

I wasn't sure what she meant by that. "It's really beautiful, but it feels more like a cage than a palace."

"Yes. That's true in a way. Some call the harem the golden cage, where we have great riches but no freedom."

12 *The Mistress of the Flowers*

Belkıs had told me that the Mistress of the Flowers spent so much time with the plants that she was gradually becoming one of them. "She can communicate with flowers and plants. They tell her how to care for them—even though the *Bostanjis* often disagree with how she does things."

"Who are the Bostanjis?"

"They are those gigantic men with bald heads and huge mustaches that you can see from a distance walking around the edges of the palace grounds. They are responsible for everything that happens inside and outside the gates of Topkapı. They protect the palace and are the guardians of the palace grounds, responsible for all the forests and public palace gardens. They are also the executioners," Belkıs added.

I shuddered at the mention of executioners. "I thought you said no men were allowed in the harem except the Padishah and his sons. I thought the girls did all the gardening."

"Under the Mistress of the Flowers, we garden only *within* the harem walls. We are responsible for all the harem gardens, which are, of course, closed to the rest of the world."

We found the Mistress of the Flowers in a very large and beautiful garden. She was preparing a large floral arrangement in autumn colors. She was very small and thin, the size of a child. Her skin was so translucent that I could see the blue veins underneath, which gave her a greenish glow. She seemed very sensitive, almost like a fragile leaf. She smiled when she saw us, and her whole face lit up.

Belkıs explained to her who I was. The Mistress of the Flowers looked at me, and I felt as if she were looking right through me. She nodded and motioned us to follow her.

We went into a greenhouse nursery that was big and beautiful and had a glass dome. The Mistress of the Flowers pointed at some drawers labeled with words that were unfamiliar to me. She then opened a drawer and pointed at the numerous bulbs inside. I almost swallowed my tongue—so many tulip bulbs!

She then took us to a plot of land that had just been turned. It smelled of manure, just like the farms near my home, and a wave of homesickness swept over me. I wanted to ask her if she wanted me to plant the bulbs here, but something stopped me. I had the impression that she did not like to speak and preferred to communicate by gestures.

Belkıs nodded and said to her, "Yes, Leyla will start working in this bed with those bulbs tomorrow, as you wish, ma'am."

Then without saying anything, the Mistress of the

Flowers touched her hand to her heart and released us.

Only after we were on our way back to the dormitories did Belkıs tell me that the Mistress of the Flowers was mute. She could not speak to people but she knew how to communicate with plants. Belkıs said that the Mistress spent most of her time alone, communing with plant spirits. People thought she was odd, but they respected her seemingly magic abilities with plants.

I did not think she was odd at all. I sensed that she was extraordinary. As a fellow gardener, I guessed that she had such an affinity for plants that she might actually prefer their world to ours. Maybe she knew instinctively the connection between plants and people. One did not always need words to communicate. I knew that I was lucky to be placed under her for my apprenticeship, and that she had chosen me to be among the tulips because she had sensed my natural affinity.

I wondered if it was the coin that the poet had given me that had brought me this luck.

13 *Harem Life*

I was assigned to one of the vast dormitories that housed fifty other girls, all acemis. I was happy that Belkıs was in the same dormitory, too, although she was one of the advanced novices. I learned that some of the other girls worked in the harem gardens, like me. Each girl had her own specialty, such as roses, medicinal herbs, or flowering trees. Some excelled in plant crafts like making silk flowers, dried bouquets and wreaths, or leaf calligraphy. Others knew how to make delicious preserves and sherbets from the essence of flowers like roses and violets. Some, like the Mistress of the Flowers, cultivated the language of flowers.

The dormitories were crowded, and we slept on mattresses on the floor that we stored in the closets during the day. There was a matron for every ten girls to make sure that we didn't get into mischief. Sometimes one of the girls would get into a fit of giggles, and then others would join in. Soon the matron's voice would rise in the dark and declare some form of punishment, such as cleaning the baths. Then everyone would quiet down.

It was in the quiet before sleep every night that I felt the most homesick. I thought of my family, hoping and praying that they were all right. I was comforted in knowing that because of me, they had enough to see them through for a while. But I wondered how Mother and Cengiz were managing the garden without me. Had the twins stopped speaking their own private twins language yet? Was Cengiz still thinking of being an artist, like Father? I also prayed for Father's safe return. And at the end of every night's prayer for my family, I breathed a special prayer for Lena—a prayer that she was safe and that we might yet find each other here in İstanbul.

I never cried, but I sometimes heard some of the other novices quietly weeping after all was quiet. Like me, they, too, must have had families they'd left behind.

Every morning we woke up with the müezzin's call to prayer. Allahüakbar! It was a lovely sound, filling the air with tenderness and reminding us to commune with the divine.

Our meals came from the royal kitchens outside the harem, then passed into the eunuchs' hall through revolving cabinets. Some girls were "tasters," because they showed characteristics that made them perfect for the job, such as total devotion and pride in self-sacrifice. Their job was to taste the food for the important ladies, in case someone tried poisoning them.

At first I thought this was silly. But I changed my mind when Ceylan, one of the tasters, began writhing on the floor and foaming at the mouth. She had just tasted the Haseki Sultana's *halvah*. The eunuchs immediately picked Ceylan up and carried her away—we assumed to the infirmary. But Ceylan never returned. I think were all privately concerned, but no one talked about it.

Finally, I asked Belkıs, "What happened to Ceylan? Where is she?"

"Shh!" she silenced me as she lowered her voice. "Some say her liver was destroyed and they sent her back to her village. But I also heard that she passed away that evening. May Allah give her peace."

In the mornings, we set up little round tables for breakfast. We had feta cheese, olives, rose jam, violet sugar, and freshly baked bread, and we ate seated cross-legged on floor cushions. Then we put the tables away and each of us went to work.

In addition to my work in the gardens, I was given lessons in the Turkish language, etiquette, and the Koran. These lessons were taught by the heads of those departments, or *odas*, which meant "rooms." The head of each department was sort of like a mother to the girls who worked in her department—

like the Mistress of the Flowers was to us.

I enjoyed my lessons and meeting girls from other departments, but I was happiest working in the gardens. Even though it was the dormant period, there was work to be done preparing the old beds for the spring and planning new beds. The Mistress of the Flowers taught us not only how to grow things but the secret language of the flowers. Each flower stood for something specific. For example, marigolds represented jealousy and periwinkles represented friendship. Magnolias were for perseverance, pomegranates were for foolishness, and yellow tulips represented hopeless love. Even trees had meaning in the language of flowers—for example, plane trees represented genius. The Mistress of the Flowers wrote down the flower names and characteristics. I learned that some people knew the language of flowers so well that they could make bouquets expressing their emotions. Sometimes they pressed flowers between the pages of the Koran and dried them in beautiful shapes, then composed flower poems. I wanted someday to be able to do the same.

The high-voiced men Belkıs had told me were called "eunuchs" were the keepers of the harem. They were the neutrals, neither men nor women. They managed the harem and acted as the messengers between the women of the harem, the Padishah, and his mother, the *Valide Sultana*—the Mother Sultana. The Chief Housekeeper assigned tasks and managed the harem girls. The *Haznedar* paid the harem expenses and "slipper money" to the girls. Although every girl within the harem was given her work clothes and food, slipper money was paid to allow girls to buy extra things, such as special fabrics and clothing, jewelry, and other adornments. These could be purchased from the bundle ladies, women merchants who sometimes visited the harem with their goods. Pensions were paid to the women who were sent to the Palace of Tears, where the ladies who were no longer part of the harem were sent. But acemis like me didn't get paid until we were more fully trained. I wondered how long that would take.

At first, I was amused by the names of the department heads, like the Mistress of the Robes, the Keeper of the Baths, the Keeper of the Jewels, the Mistress of the Sherbets, the Reader of the Koran, the Chief Coffee-maker, the Keeper of Lingerie, the Mistress of the Flowers, the Mistress of Maladies, and other titles like that. But slowly I came to understand how intricately they worked together.

Belkıs and I started a game of noting the name of everyone whose face we knew. We played it whenever we worked together in the gardens.

"How many women are in the harem?" I asked her.

"There are supposed to be one thousand."

"What about the new girls arriving from all over the empire?" Almost every week new girls were brought in. Even though I was still considered an acemi, I no longer felt like one of the new ones.

"After they are trained, they are assigned to one of the several palaces of the Padishah. He always moves from one palace to another, depending on the season and his whim. His fortune grows. We are part of his treasure, the symbol of his wealth. The more women a man has, the richer he is." Her face brightened as she said this, as if she was impressed with all this.

"I bet you wouldn't mind being an *odalisque*, Belkıs," I said.

"There's not a chance of that, my friend," she said wistfully.

The most beautiful and talented girls competed to become personal odalisques. A dozen of them served the Padishah—they bathed, shaved, and dressed him, brought his food, did his personal laundry, played music, and danced for him. Others read poetry and practiced flirtation.

The Padishah had several wives and sometimes girlfriends that were called his "favorites." All of them competed to have sons and be the next Mother Sultana, who was truly the ruler of the harem. She had her own pavilions and handmaidens. Her power in the harem and in the whole empire was enormous. The eunuchs took orders from her. Even the Padishah kissed her hand and paid her a daily visit. He took her advice on almost everything.

"The world lies at the foot of the mother," he was heard to proclaim.

The Haseki Sultana, or first wife, was the next in

the pecking order. She would hesitate at nothing to keep her position, if anything threatened it—including, I was told, getting rid of her rivals or their children.

The Padishah sometimes gave some of the odalisques as gifts or in marriage to his rich and powerful Pashas. When that happened, the odalisques left and became mistresses of their own homes.

But the rest of us were here to stay forever—unless, I learned, the Padishah passed away. Then all of his harem would be sent to that palace of the unwanted ones called the Palace of Tears. It was said to be a palace full of sad women. Some quiet nights we could hear their weeping. I prayed I would never end up in that sad place.

Some girls in the harem were nice but others were not. There were power struggles even at the level of the acemis. If you were a loner, you were harassed. One time one of the girls got into my closet and made a mess of the few things I had. The girl and her group laughed, but it was hurtful, not funny.

"You have to become part of a clique and ally

yourself with a group. It's the only way to protect yourself within the dormitory," Belkıs explained. "But never trust anyone fully."

"Even you?"

"Even me," she laughed. "*Except* me, of course, silly girl."

Belkıs had been brought to the harem from another town in Georgia. Maybe it was because we had experienced so many of the same things, had smelled the same air, known the same sounds, and remembered a similar life in our earlier worlds, that we could so often read each other's minds without saying anything. She was like a sister to me.

Despite the competition, backbiting, and gossip, there was some real affection among the girls. Most of them were usually warm and generous. They sometimes shared their clothes with one another or braided one another's hair while sharing beauty tips and gossip. We spent our free time together talking and playing games. We played music and danced. I soon became comfortable in the baths, too, where we were able to relax, play in the pools, and talk freely.

After all, we were all sharing the same destiny.

Slowly, as autumn slipped into winter and I learned to find my way around that beautiful place, I came to regard the other girls as my new family. I had never had sisters, and in this world of women, I found something sweet and nourishing. I still missed my own family, but I came to understand what that eunuch had told me: "Once you pass through the Gate of Felicity, there is no going back." We would all spend the rest of our lives here. That was our destiny.

14 *Winter*

It snowed that winter. Everyone said this was unusual in İstanbul. Some of us still had to work in the greenhouses and others in the sheltered winter garden courtyard but never outside in the regular harem garden beds. The gardens mostly slept in the winter.

I was secretly glad of the snow, for I knew how good the frozen earth would be for the tulips under my care.

I also did some experimentation. I heated some of the bulbs, then moistened and combined them with others by a sort of grafting, a small and delicate manipulation. Then I put them away until spring, shut up to rest in cold and darkness.

I had planted many of the bulbs that the Mistress of the Flowers had assigned to me in a patch that I had also planted with a forget-me-not border interspersed with narcissus and jonquil bulbs. Among the other tulips, three of my own bulbs were hidden, their positions marked so that I could keep track. I was nervous someone would discover that I had planted my own bulbs, but I prayed that nobody would notice them before the petals opened.

I was still taking lessons, but with the gardens inactive I had more free time, and I missed the painting and sketching that I used to do. The beauty of the palace was inspiring, and I found myself making small ink sketches without realizing it during my lessons. The *imam* constantly reminded us to learn and abide by the word of Allah. I knew that it was forbidden to draw anything that looked like people, animals, or plants. Father and Cengiz and I had frequently discussed this, and Father always repeated that his gift was also the work of Allah, so he painted everything. It made sense to me, but I had come to understand that to do the kind of painting I most loved would be a problem here. So I kept my mouth shut and never mentioned painting after that first day, when I had spoken of it to the Chief Housekeeper.

The weather was not nearly as cold as where I came from. Even so, we acemis spent our days indoors trying to keep warm, telling stories or reading fortunes from coffee grounds, staying warm by keeping our feet near the *tandırs* under the tables. We were well-fed—we had lots and lots of pilaf and lamb and syrupy desserts and cookies. We saw even fancier dishes delivered to the royal ladies in their private apartments within the harem—desserts like *baklava* and beautiful desserts with funny names like Lady's Fingers, The Padishah's Delight, or Lips of the Beauty. But after Ceylan's death from eating the Haseki Sultana's halvah, I had little interest in trying any of these dishes.

The windows behind the lattices had frost on the inside. The royal ladies wore furs such as sable and ermine to stay warm, but we girls had nothing so grand. We slept with scarves on our heads to stay warm. A cough or the croup would send us to the infirmary, where it was warmer and we could stay in comfortable beds with someone to take care of us. The Mistress of Maladies was a kind lady originally from Macedonia who liked me because I occasionally brought her special herbs from the gardens. Her kindness was comforting, but it also made me feel very lonely, because it reminded me of how much I missed my mother.

My education continued and I progressed rapidly. In addition to learning court etiquette and how to speak properly, I memorized and learned to recite poetry. And I learned more of the prayers in the Koran.

When the müezzin chanted from his minaret five times a day, all of us in the palace stopped what we were doing. We pulled out our prayer rugs and performed the *namaz*, bending and unbending as we faced west toward the holy city of Mecca. Every day I prayed to Allah that my mother and brothers were surviving the winter and that my father would return home, as he had in my first dream here. I prayed for little Lena. Even as I settled in to my life in the harem and felt happy to be learning so many new things, I prayed for a miracle, for my family to reunite someday, somehow. Although I knew it was impossible, I still couldn't stop myself from hoping. There was something so mysterious and powerful about the müezzin's song that it always made me feel peaceful and hopeful. Allahüakbar. God is great.

As far as I knew, everyone in the whole city stopped to pray five times a day, too, to be reminded of the great spiritual power that united everyone. There is only one Allah. No other God but God.

15 *The Royal Halvet*

At the beginning of March, the crocuses and narcissus began to sprout, and with each bud came promise. Jonquils and hyacinths followed. Finally, the fruit trees burst forth with blossoms that filled the air with their sweet scents.

The Bostanjis came into the harem gardens and uncovered another large square area. The ground was laid out in beds of loam mixed with river mud, and each bed was surrounded by a border of turf to keep the soil in place. I had planted my bulbs in a fairly shady area to temper the noonday heat, and water was in abundant supply. I was now constantly weeding, working in manure, and watering all my beds, but with special attention to my tulips. I knelt on the turf border, meditating on the forces that might be affected by crossing colors. The tulips were constantly on my mind. Even my dreams were full of tulips. I had become crazy for tulips, just like the Dutch people old Ilia had told me about.

I worked alone a lot, but sometimes the Mistress of the Flowers appeared, as if from out of nowhere. She stood and watched me. I wondered if she knew that I had mixed in my own bulbs and that I had been experimenting with them. And if she did, what would she do?

When the snow melted, the Chief Housekeeper announced that there would soon be a *halvet*, a private celebration for the royal family, to welcome the first day of spring. All the Bostanjis and the gardeners were called out to work and prepare the gardens. We trimmed branches and raked the grass so that everything in the garden was serene and orderly. Soon there was not even a leaf to be seen on the lawn. We adjusted the stones to tune the fountains and added moss to balance the music of the running water. The Bostanjis brought out large cages with colorful birds of all kinds—parrots, cockatoos, macaws, and parakeets—birds that I'd never seen until I came to İstanbul. Peacocks and birds of paradise wandered freely among the shrubs. The garden was *cennet*, paradise, the garden of Allah.

On the first day of spring, the royal family, including all of the Sultan's wives and favorites, plus the Princes and the Princesses, were to promenade and enjoy themselves in the palace gardens that we had so carefully prepared. I wished to see it all, but the acemis were not allowed to participate. Still, I couldn't contain my curiosity. It was a big risk, but I had to see for myself the royals in their finery in our gardens.

As the other gardeners finished their last touches of preparation for the halvet, I slipped away. Next to the wall was a small space behind a sycamore that I'd started training to grow in the shape of a fan. I slipped in and tried to get comfortable while I waited. I knew that if I got caught, it could be the end of me. My heart was racing so, I thought it might burst out of my body. If I was found, what would happen to me? How would I be punished? Yet my fear was less than the curiosity that had led me here.

I watched every step and every aspect of the final preparations, amazed again at the effort and exactitude of all that was being done. Late in the morning, a corps of eunuchs arrived and laid fancy carpets on the grass. I still puzzled over the eunuchs, how it was that they were not men, but I was now accustomed to seeing them in the harem. After the eunuchs, odalisques came out carrying all sorts of wonderful food and sweets displayed with utmost opulence. Then parasols and canopies were set in place, and more carpets and cushions were laid out. Then came the lady musicians and singers. Settling themselves on a dais, they began to play music, the like of which I had never heard.

A procession began as the eunuchs cleared the way

for the Valide Sultana, the mother of the Padishah. Her skin was very pale, as was fashionable, and her cheeks were painted red. She was dripping with emeralds and pearls. Some of the odalisques held a canopy over her head to protect her from the sun.

Alongside the Sultana walked a pear-shaped eunuch. He leaned down and whispered something to her. It was the man who had bought me from Madam Siranush! Sümbül Ağa—Master Hyacinth. I had not seen him since that fated day at the market. I had assumed he was just an agent who had sold me to the palace. But here he was, so close to the most powerful woman in the empire. Obviously, he himself was someone very important.

After the Valide Sultana was settled, what must have been the other wives came out with their own odalisques, eunuchs, and children. There were girls and boys not much older than I, and all were dressed in such beautiful clothes. Since the garden was completely walled off and no one would be able to see their faces, the women were unveiled. Some reclined on divans under silk tents. The older ladies wore warm tunics with fur collars and fur hats.

As the royal family enjoyed the piles of figs and grapes set out before them, musicians and singing girls came out to perform. The odalisques danced and sang songs filled with yearning. Everyone feasted on sherbets that someone had told me were made with snow brought from Mt. Olympus.

This part of the harem's world of women I had never seen before. I had never seen so many beautiful ladies all at once. These were the privileged ones, and they looked it as they sat celebrating the arrival of spring. They existed in a world of their own, a world filled with beauty and ease that I longed to be a part of. Instead, my world was filled with orders and work—work that made the halvet possible for the royal family to enjoy. It was odd to think of this, to realize how our worlds were both so different and so connected.

A boy in a maroon vest caught my attention. Over his vest was a fancy brocade tunic that reached the ground, and he wore a white turban with a jeweled *aigrette*. An elaborately carved scabbard at his waist held a *scimitar*. He looked a couple of years older than I, and he seemed both very serious and alert to everything that was going on around him. It was as if he expected constant danger. On his shoulder perched a handsome falcon, just as alert. The boy himself reminded me of a falcon—it was as if his eyes noticed everything.

Then I noticed a girl about my own age dressed in a royal blue gown, who was holding the hand of a little girl dressed just like her. I watched as they crossed the lawn and sat down. She cradled the child as if she were a doll and began braiding her hair. I heard the child giggling and caught my breath. As I watched, the child turned around and I saw to my amazement that it was Lena! My Lena! Even though we were far apart, our destinies had brought us to the same place once again. I was filled with a sense of gratitude and peace I could not name.

But it didn't last long. Someone suddenly grabbed my arm and covered my mouth so I could not scream. When I turned, I saw that it was the serious boy, the Prince who had been carrying the falcon.

"Who are you and what are you doing here?" he

demanded roughly.

I was not wearing a veil, so I tried to cover my face with my free hand. "Please! Let go! You're hurting me," I said quietly. I did not want to draw anyone else's attention.

"Not unless you answer my question," he said sternly, but I noticed he, too, was using a quiet voice.

I nodded and he let go of me. I held my apron across my face, since he was a stranger. Girls here were not supposed to reveal their faces to men other than close relatives.

"I . . . I work in the garden, sir," I said tentatively.

"You're not supposed to be here right now. Nobody is, except the royal family."

"Yes, I know that," I said, looking down at the grass. I did not want to seem disrespectful.

"Then why are you here? Surely you must know the rules."

"Because . . . because, sir, I wanted to see the halvet with my own eyes. I had heard how beautiful it was here on the first day of spring, in the garden, in the sun. I wanted to see the ladies. I . . . I wanted to see the whole beautiful scene."

He shook his head as if he was disapproving, but I sensed a softening. "You're a silly girl. I guess nothing is really wrong with that desire unless, of course, you're lying. I'll let you go this time and won't tell anyone. But I never want to see you here again, or anywhere else you are not supposed to be, no matter how much you want it. Do you understand? Anywhere! Or I'll have to cut off your head. Be gone now!" He sounded very fierce again. He grabbed the scabbard of his scimitar.

I hurried back to the conservatory, where I found Belkıs looking for me. My heart was pounding. My face was flushed.

"What's the matter with you? Where have you been?" she asked. "I've been looking for you everywhere."

I told her where I'd been and what I'd seen.

"Why do you take such chances, Leyla? You don't realize what could happen to you if you break the rules here. It's very dangerous! But now that you're all right, tell me what else happened and what you saw." I could see that she was curious, too.

I told her about all that I'd seen—the royal family in their beautiful clothes. I told her about the dazzling Valide Sultana and Master Hyacinth. And I told her about the Prince who had found me and threatened me. Maybe I shouldn't have. Maybe I shouldn't have told anyone that I had secretly watched the royal halvet. Belkıs was the one who had warned me to keep things to myself in the harem. She'd said that secrets could be used against a person. I was beginning to feel afraid. But I knew that she would never talk of my misdeed to someone else. She was my friend.

"The Valide is a very clever lady," Belkıs explained, "and her son, our Padishah, worships her. As for the boy, he must be Prince Mejnun, the Padishah's youngest son. They say that his head is always in the clouds and that he is a philosopher."

"How do you know all this?" I asked. Belkıs constantly surprised me with all she knew.

"When I used to be in the service of the Haseki Sultana, I heard all the gossip about the royal family."

"But he was going to kill me, Belkıs!" I said.

She laughed. "No, Prince Mejnun does not have a

mean bone in his body. They say he has no ambition for running an empire, either. He is a lover of peace like his father, but he will never be a Padishah. Prince Mejnun believes that all problems can be solved by mutual respect. He must have been teasing you when he threatened you."

"Well, he didn't show me much mutual respect. It was just the opposite. He really scared me," I told her.

"You should be glad you're still alive, Leyla! He could have turned you in if he had wanted to. But obviously, he didn't. You're very, very lucky. If one of the eunuchs had found you . . ."

Then I told her the best part, about seeing Lena and the Princess with the beautiful dress who was holding Lena's hand and braiding her hair.

"Did she have large green eyes?" Belkıs asked.

"The Princess? Yes, I think she did."

"That must have been Princess Fatma, then. And your Lena most likely is Semiramis, her living doll. I heard one of the odalisques talking about them."

This wasn't making sense to me. "But . . . how can a person be a doll?"

"Some of the ladies in the court are given little girls as gifts and they turn them into living dolls—like playthings. But human playthings."

This was hard for me to understand. A living doll? "What happens when the Princess is too old to play with the doll anymore?"

"That depends on the mistress. Some are very nice and treat the living dolls like their own children."

"And when the dolls grow up?"

"Oh, that also depends on the mistress. The living dolls usually remain with their mistresses all their lives. Poor Princess Fatma. I'm glad she has a distraction. She is so young and already a widow." Belkıs sighed in sympathy.

"A widow!" I exclaimed. "But she's—"

"They married her to an old Pasha when she was five. Her husband was away fighting in a war against Hungary and lost his life. So she became a widow."

"But that's impossible. How could anyone that young be married? Lena's five years old, and look at how little she is!"

"The age doesn't matter. The marriage was just

symbolic anyway, at the beginning. Not for real. In such cases, the couple is not expected to live together in the same house as husband and wife until the girl becomes a woman."

I wondered when it was exactly that a girl became a woman, ready to be the wife of an old man.

"There are rumors that she'll be married again soon," Belkıs continued.

"To whom?"

"To the Sultan's Grand Vizier himself, İbrahim Pasha," Belkıs smiled. "He is very powerful."

"But the Pasha is also much older, is he not?" I'd heard some of the girls talking about the Grand Vizier.

"He's not really that old. Besides, he's the most enlightened person in the empire. He's brilliant and very rich. They say he is the real mind behind the Padishah, he gives him advice on everything. He is the Padishah's closest ally."

Belkıs went on to tell me that the Padishah was very fortunate to have a Grand Vizier like İbrahim Pasha. İbrahim loved the best things in life as much as the Padishah did. They had been close friends since the

Padishah was a Prince. It was widely said that İbrahim read the Padishah's soul as if he were looking at a mirror. "The Padishah wanted him to become his Vizier many times, but İbrahim Pasha refused. I can understand why. Most Grand Viziers have lost their heads for making wrong decisions. İbrahim Pasha was too smart to be the next. But finally the Sultan convinced him."

"What made him change his mind?" I asked, wondering again at how much Belkıs knew.

"They say he saw the unimaginable horror of war and made up his mind to find an end to it. He is a man of peace. So he returned to İstanbul to dissuade the Padishah from continuing the war."

"And now he shall marry Princess Fatma?"

"That's what I've heard. Of course, the Pasha already has several other wives and children." Belkıs was just getting warmed up.

"I know the Padishah has many wives, but is that true of all men?" I couldn't imagine my father marrying other women besides my mother.

"Any man is allowed to marry as many as four wives; the Padishahs, as many as they want." Belkıs shrugged.

"But how can any girl be happy with such an older man? They'd have nothing in common." I thought of Princess Fatma and how young she looked. My age.

"It's an honor bestowed upon the Grand Vizier. It shows that the Padishah is willing to mix his blood with İbrahim Pasha's, that he accepts him as part of his family."

"But what about the Princess? Do you think *she* wants to marry İbrahim Pasha?" I was really struggling to make sense of it all.

"The Princesses have more freedom than other women. They can live outside the harem and are still considered more powerful than their husbands," Belkıs went on. "And İbrahim Pasha is well respected, besides. It's a good arrangement for Princess Fatma."

I was exhausted that night from all the excitement, but I could not sleep. I kept thinking about all that I'd seen and heard. What if Belkıs was wrong? What if Prince Mejnun was serious about cutting off my head? And I was most disturbed by the thought of the Princess marrying such an older man, even one as illustrious as İbrahim Pasha, who already had other wives and children. But most of all, I thought about Lena. I was relieved to have seen her happy and well cared for. *There are probably worse things than being a living doll*, I thought. *And at least the Princess seemed kind and loving with Lena. Maybe Lena will be all right.*

The Padishah spent the winters in Topkapı Palace. I learned that by the time the fruit trees had lost their blossoms, he usually took some of his pages and part of the harem, including eunuchs and his children, and moved to a different palace. But that spring, he remained in Topkapı Palace.

"The rumor is that the Padishah is planning to build a new palace on the Sweet Waters of Asia," Belkıs told me.

"The Sweet Waters of Asia?" I asked.

"That is the confluence of the two streams falling into the Golden Horn—the narrow inlet of water your ship probably traveled through coming to İstanbul," Belkıs explained. "That's where people go to party, promenade, and picnic. They go rowing their beautiful *cäiques*. They say that the Padishah is building a new palace there because he wants to be in the middle of all that entertainment."

Belkıs told me that İstanbul was known as the city of peace and enlightenment. She said the Padishah loved art and poetry and had a passion for tulips. He was committed to enjoying life to its maximum, to living fully every moment and savoring the good things in life. He also wished the same for his subjects. Some said he even wanted his enemies to enjoy life—although he was known to claim that he had no enemies.

The Padishah was friendly with the countries in Europe, the heathen lands to the west. He sent his own ambassadors to Europe and invited theirs to İstanbul. He made a point of getting to know these foreigners and becoming friends with them.

"Our cultures can learn from each other. Instead of being at war, we could trade ideas and resources," he was reported to have told them.

Some of his subjects worshipped the Padishah and İbrahim Pasha, while others whispered unhappily that ever since the Padishah had come to power, all the wars had stopped and people did not fight each other anymore. It was mainly the *Janissaries*, who were special soldiers, who were unhappy with the long period of peace. They were men bred for war, and now they couldn't fight. As one who knew what war could do to a family, I was glad to know that the Padishah had stopped fighting wars. That meant that the people of my old country, including my family, could live in peace.

16 *The Most Beautiful Clothes*

Master Hyacinth had become the Chief Eunuch and he announced one day that the Padishah wanted to meet his entire harem in *Hunkar Sofasi*, the Hall of the Sultan, that very day. We were all going to be individually introduced to the mighty Padishah.

All the girls in the harem were very excited and started talking about what they would wear and what they might say if the Padishah spoke to them—all, that is, except me. I had nothing to wear besides my work clothes, and I didn't think it would be respectful to go before the Padishah in dirty or soiled clothing. To hide my disappointment and block out the excited chatter all around me, I ran out to the garden and began working on my tulip beds. I picked dead leaves from plants to try to distract myself.

I heard Belkıs calling me, so I went inside, trying to hide my distress. All the girls were dressing up, excited and happy. Everyone was talking about the audience with the Sultan.

"What's the matter with you, Leyla? Why aren't you dressed yet? Master Hyacinth will be here any minute, you know. Do you want to be left behind?" she scolded me.

"I'm not going," I told her, somewhat defiantly.

"But our Padishah wants to see everyone. Even *you* are not an exception."

"I can't go," I said stubbornly.

"Why not?" Belkıs clearly had no idea.

"I have nothing to wear." I strained to keep from bursting into tears.

Belkıs realized I was telling the truth. "Oh, Leyla. I wish I had another nice outfit I could loan you, but I don't. I only have an extra pair of silk *şalvar*. That's all."

"I have a chemise," said another girl, who had been listening as she dressed nearby. "You may borrow it, if you like."

"And I have a yashmak," said another girl, one whose smile always lightened my heart. "You're certainly welcome to it."

Suddenly I was surrounded by the girls who had befriended me. They started pulling all sorts of clothes, scarves, and jewelry out of the closets. They removed my work clothes and dressed me as if I were a doll. They even braided my hair with pearls after painting my eyes with kohl and putting rouge on my cheeks. I resisted a little at first, uncomfortable with so many of them lavishing attention on me. But they cooed with each addition, and it soon became fun.

When they stopped, and I saw my reflection in the looking glass, I gasped. This couldn't be me!

I wore a pair of baggy trousers of shimmering red silk with a sheer white blouse whose fashionably long sleeves were edged with Damascus lace. Over it all I wore a kaftan of the finest silk brocade edged with gold trim and tied with a tasseled cord in the front. My hotoz was covered with a red translucent veil, pulled together with a gold and emerald brooch. One of the girls had loaned me a pair of dangling emerald earrings and a gold bracelet set with a ruby. Around my neck someone had placed two long strands of pearls. Finally, I wore the softest yellow leather slippers embroidered with tulips, just as if they'd been made especially for me. At the last moment, Belkıs stuck a fan in my hands.

How could this elegant girl possibly be me, the girl named Laleena who had run wild in the Caucasus not so long ago? This girl in the looking glass resembled a Princess! With a grateful smile, I looked around at all the girls, all of whom also looked magnificent. Surely, the Padishah would be pleased with such a harem!

17 *The Hall of the Sultan*

We were escorted into the Hall of the Sultan. It was the first time that I'd been in that part of the palace. This enormous room was more beautiful than any other part of the palace. A stained glass dome scattered colored light everywhere. The windows faced the Golden Horn and opened out onto a grand terrace.

Through the windows I was stunned to see what surrounded us. I had had no idea before where Topkapı Palace was located, even though I was living in it. I had been taken from Madam Siranush's house and through the Gate of Felicity without having seen where I was. The harbor and the enclosed world of the harem was all that I'd seen of İstanbul. My heart was beating rapidly at the sight of such beauty and grandeur. This had to be some sort of a magic kingdom. Green hills were framed by cypresses and linden trees. The city looked as if it were carved out of jasper. I noticed that some of the other girls were just as awed as I was. But I was also confused. Why did we women have to live in such seclusion? Why were we separated from the rest of the world? I hungered to explore further, to see what else this place had in store for me.

My attention was soon drawn to the man at the center of the room. This was the first time that I'd seen the Padishah. He was sitting on a golden throne, dressed in a magnificent *kaftan* of green silk embroidered with golden tulips. His turban had an aigrette with an enormous tear-shaped emerald that was surrounded by rubies and diamonds. Underneath his diamond-studded sash hung a silver dagger, its sheath inlaid with more emeralds and rubies.

Behind him I recognized his mother, the Valide Sultana, who seemed solemn and dignified.

My eyes moved around the room. I saw faces that were familiar from the harem and I recognized some of the royalty from the halvet. The Padishah's wives sat on a separate dais, along with their daughters. Out of his twenty-four children, only the names of a few Princesses were called out by Master Hyacinth: Atika, Hatice, Ummu-Gulsum, Saliha, Zeynep, Ayse, Emetullah, Safiye, Emine, and Fatma. I searched for Princess Fatma, hoping that I might again see Lena, but I couldn't find them in the crowd.

As we arrived, we saluted and formed lines around the Padishah according to our rank. One by one, each of us approached the throne and kissed the skirt of his kaftan. He nodded and made eye contact with each of us. I was very nervous, but as I watched the other girls going first, I decided that the Padishah was indeed a gentle and kindly man. Sometimes he stopped a girl to ask her name. Sometimes he recognized an old nurse or an odalisque and asked after her health.

After we had all greeted him and had settled down, he looked around the room and addressed us. "Nothing gives me more pleasure than to have all my harem, all my ladies, in the same room. Welcome. I want you all to enjoy yourselves fully."

The Padishah then escorted us all out onto the enormous terrace of marble and pointed at the confluence of the two waters. "That unfinished structure you see on the opposite shore?" he said, pointing. "It will soon be a new palace and will be the most magnificent palace in the world. More poetic than Topkapı. More splendid than the palaces built by our eastern ancestors. More opulent than even the French king's palace called Versailles."

Belkıs had told me that the Padishah was fascinated with the lifestyles of France's kings, as well as with their palaces and fountains. The drawings of the palaces and fancy objects sent from France thrilled him.

"But this new palace has a much lovelier setting than any other. It will have colored tiles trimmed with gold. The finest craftsmen and the best artisans and artists from all over the world have worked on it. I will call it *Sad-a-bad*, the 'palace of happiness.' It will be the shining star among the other palaces and gardens along the Golden Horn. Someday, you too will enjoy its pleasures. You will hear the music of heaven on earth.

"We will inaugurate Sadabad in honor of the wedding of my daughter Princess Fatma to the Grand Vizier İbrahim Pasha and the manhood ceremonies of two of my sons. Everything will coincide with this year's Tulip Festival."

All faces turned to Princess Fatma, and I finally spotted her—and Lena—among the rest of the royal family. She cast her eyes down as she sat on a special throne holding Lena like a baby. But I could tell that Lena was restless. She was squirming and looking around, and she seemed ready to climb out of the Princess's arms at any moment.

Suddenly Lena saw me, and her eyes met mine. I tried to shake my head to tell her not to move, but with a swift movement, she jumped down from the Princess's lap and ran toward me. She grabbed hold of my legs; then she reached up and opened her arms, silently asking to be lifted up. All eyes were on me now and I didn't know what to do. Swiftly, one of the Princess's attendants came over and took Lena back to the Princess. Lena looked back at me and began to cry.

"What you have done puts me to shame, Semiramis," I heard the Princess say to Lena. "You should never call attention to yourself around our Padishah." She whispered something to her attendant, who took the child out of the room.

Semiramis. That's what they call Lena now, I thought. *My little Lena is now Semiramis, just as Laleena is now Leyla.*

Master Hyacinth signaled the musicians to play, to distract the royal party from this disruption. The music began and dancers came out, clacking their wooden spoons as they whirled. The music was wonderful, but I was still distracted by what had just happened with Lena. I worried that it would bring trouble to both of us. While the dancers danced on, food was served, and we were allowed to eat. But I had no appetite. Once again, Lena had been snatched away from me.

After the feast and the entertainment, the Padishah stood up, and the evening was over. As we saluted him, he stopped on his way out and dropped his handker-chief in front of Belkıs, then left through the door leading to the Golden Road—the corridor that connected the *selamlık*, his private quarters, to the harem. The whole room fell silent. We all knew what the dropping of the handkerchief meant.

18 *The Secret Paintings*

The next day, the Mistress of the House summoned Belkıs. I was waiting for her when she back came out into the corridor.

"She told me that it's true, that the Padishah has chosen me to be one of his odalisques," Belkıs told me breathlessly.

"I guess we all knew that when he dropped the handkerchief in front of you. Praise be to Allah! That is such good news for you!" I hugged her.

Even though I was happy for Belkıs, I felt a confusion of feelings. I knew this was what she had wished for. Most of the girls in the harem did. She would now be moved into private quarters and be given her own attendant and eunuch. She could have beautiful dresses and jewels. And if the Padishah favored her, she even had the potential of becoming a Sultana someday. But it also meant that her life in the harem would now be separate from mine, and I was sad to lose my friend.

It seemed to be my destiny to part with everyone I loved—first my father, then my mother and brothers, then little Lena, and now Belkıs.

Belkis had been my mentor, my protector, and my teacher in the harem. I had other friends now as well, but no one could take her place. Before she moved to her separate quarters, I wanted to give her a gift so she would not forget me. But as an acemi, I had next to nothing. What could I possibly give her that would be special and unusual? Since tulip season was so close, I thought that perhaps I could give her a special tulip. But tulips were ephemeral—they didn't last. They also didn't dry well. I needed to find something more durable and everlasting.

The next morning, I encountered a minor miracle. I was on my way to the conservatory when I saw some discarded sheets of paper that someone had used to practice her calligraphy. The other sides of the paper were blank and usable. It was as if they were taunting me, begging to have something drawn on them.

My impulse was to keep them, of course, rather than have them thrown into the fire and wasted. Father had taught us to respect paper because trees gave up their lives for it. I realized that I could be accused of theft, but I took the paper anyway and hid it behind the heavy tapestries on the walls leading to the Hall of the Sultan.

Later, I stopped at the laundry to drop off some things. Dyes were prepared in the same building. I watched as a woman stirred yellow dye into a vat of blue, and the color turned green before my eyes. It so powerfully reminded me of the magic of mixing colors with Father that my breath caught in my throat. As I watched, I made up my mind.

"I'm here to get some primary colors," I told her. "Yellow, blue, and red." They were the basis of all colors, and I knew that by mixing them, I could create all the other colors. Father had instructed Cengiz and me on how to mix colors, as well as what plants and materials to use to extract colors—like madder for red, sumac for purple, and lobster shells for deep orange.

"What do you need them for?" the woman asked.

"I'm not told," I answered.

"Who are they for?" Was she suspicious of me?

"For the Chief Housekeeper," I made up. My heart was beating wildly.

But the woman seemed not to notice my discomfort. She measured some dyes in powder form and put them into separate parchment envelopes. I thanked her and left, and then I hid the dyes in the greenhouse, among some potions we used for gardening. I had the paint-brushes I'd brought from home, and I took charcoal from one of the fires.

I had taken paper that was not mine and had lied to get the dyes for my colors, and I was determined to paint. Now the challenge was finding a place and the time to do it. I was always with others. I slept in the dormitory with the rest of the acemis. I had my meals with them. I bathed with them. I worked with the other gardeners in the garden. I was almost never alone for more than a few seconds. But occasionally there were moments when others strayed. Or they just stopped noticing. That was the time to slip away.

I found a place by the gazebo near the tulip beds. As my gift for Belkıs, I wanted to draw the tulips in different stages of their cycle—from the time that the pale seed sprouts began to peep from the ground to their wilting back into the earth.

That first day, I was so absorbed in my drawing that I was not aware of the Mistress of the Flowers watching me. She looked at the sketch and smiled a meaningful smile that I wasn't sure how to interpret. Then she drifted off into another part of the garden.

I immediately hid the drawings underneath the floorboards of the gazebo, praying that no one would find them. What was the Mistress of the Flowers going to do now that she had seen me drawing? Would she turn me in? Would my drawings be where I had hidden them when I returned?

I avoided my hiding place for a couple of days, fearing that someone else might be watching me. But when I returned a few days later, the drawings were there, just as I'd left them. I examined the tulips in my garden to see how the closed petals concealed the hidden treasures of the tulip chalice, and I drew that. I was happy to be drawing and painting again, even though I knew I was once again risking everything. By now I trusted the Mistress of the Flowers, so I thought I was safe. However, unbeknownst to me, I was being watched by someone else.

When I next returned to the drawings, I could tell that they had been moved. I found a note written in beautiful calligraphy attached to them with simply the words, "Beauty never vanishes, but is transformed." Were these the words of the Mistress of the Flowers? Who else could have left this for me?

Finally, over a series of days filled with stolen moments, I completed Belkıs's gift. I felt a strange sensation as I looked at the drawings, something mysterious and vivid. Was it because they reminded me so much of Father and my brother Cengiz?

At first Belkıs was speechless when she received my gift. Then she found her voice. "You are so nice to me, my dear friend," she said. "No one has ever given me a present before. But Leyla, you know that I will have to hide them because it's against our faith to make or have such paintings."

"But do you *like* them?" I had to know.

"I love them," she replied. But I could see that she was a little uneasy.

"Now the tulips are immortal," I said. "They will live forever in these drawings and as long as their images last in your mind."

"Like our friendship," Belkıs said with a catch in her throat. "Oh, I'll miss you so much. You are truly like a sister to me." She hesitated, then handed the drawings back to me. "But I can't accept these, Leyla. It's too dangerous—especially to someone in my position. As an odalisque, I must be very careful and watch my behavior every second. You never know if or when they might search my apartment."

She was telling the truth. Or maybe she sensed something about the future. I knew that she was already aspiring to be a favorite, to become a Sultana. She could no longer take risks. I told her I understood, but I still felt hurt inside. How could she *not* keep the gift that I had worked so hard to make for her? That I didn't understand.

After Balkis left the acemis' dormitory, I hid the drawings and kept to myself. I didn't want to risk getting hurt again, losing my heart to someone and then losing her. It hurt too much.

19 *The Dark Prison*

I turned to painting to find solace and comfort. Whenever I could, I returned to my secret place and made new images. But soon I was out of paints again, so I returned to the dyeing room.

"You say that the Chief Housekeeper wants *more* dyes?" the Mistress of Colors asked in a snappish voice.

"Yes, ma'am. Only the primaries."

She looked intently into my eyes. "Don't you work in the garden? I don't know why you are running errands for the Chief Housekeeper. Why didn't she send one of the girls of her own oda?"

"I don't know, ma'am."

She prepared the colors and put them into parchment envelopes. As she handed them to me, she said something under her breath that I did not understand.

But I did not like the tone of her voice.

Later that afternoon, as I was in the conservatory transplanting some seedlings into new pots, one of the young eunuchs rushed in looking for me.

"The Chief Housekeeper wants to see you immediately. She seemed very upset. What mischief are you into?" he asked.

"I can't say," I said as I brushed soil from my hands.

"You're amazing, Leyla." He shook his head. "Such a determined girl! But it's not smart to test your boundaries here in the harem, you know."

As I entered her apartment, the Chief Housekeeper was sitting on a divan, smoking her nargileh, just like the first time I'd met her, the day I became Leyla. Sitting next to her was the Mistress of Colors. I no longer had to guess why I had been summoned.

"Tell me what you have been getting the dyes for," the Chief Housekeeper said firmly.

I froze. I was silent.

"Well, they certainly were not for me," she continued. "Even though you've claimed they were."

"I'm sorry," I said.

"What were you doing with those dyes?"

What could I say? I certainly couldn't tell her about the paintings. I knew she would see them as an act of sacrilege. "I was going to add them to the soil—" I started to say.

"What for?" she demanded, interrupting me.

"To see if they affect the colors of the flowers." That's what came out of my mouth. The two women looked at each other. They did not seem convinced.

"Then why didn't you get permission from me first?"

"I was afraid you might say no, ma'am."

"This is too much, and I don't believe you." She was clearly annoyed. She took a long slurp out of her water pipe, making gurgling sounds. "That's enough misbehavior. I'm sending you to the prison for not getting permission, for lying, and for being so insolent. You will remain there until the Tulip Festival is over."

"Here is a potion I've prepared," the Mistress of Colors said. "Swallow it now, before you leave."

She told me to open my mouth and shoveled in a spoonful of red paste. I was sure she was poisoning me, yet I had no choice. I opened my mouth and very quickly gulped it down. Just as quickly, I jumped up with pain. My mouth, throat, and insides were burning. I was on fire. She had fed me hot cayenne pepper! I choked and tried to spit it out.

"It's to clean your mouth so that you won't lie again."

Once again I entered a dark world. The prison was a small room with no windows. The floor was covered with straw. It was cold and damp, and it smelled of mold and other horrible things. Through the walls, I heard the voices of other girls who were in other cells. Who were they? What had they done? How long had they been here? When was someone going to let me out?

I cried until no more tears came. I scratched imaginary drawings and carved things on the walls to keep myself sane. I could not keep track of the passing of time because I could not see the sun to orient myself. It was dark even when they brought me food. I might have been there for a few hours or a few weeks; I could not tell. What if they kept me here forever? What if no one ever came for me?

I prayed to Allah for comfort and strength.

I thought back to my family through those long hours, and my only comfort was in knowing that, because of me, Mother and Cengiz and the twins had enough for a long time. And maybe by now Father had returned, and they would be better cared for. I was still trying to be optimistic.

I wondered why it was considered so wrong to make paintings of things like flowers or even people. In my heart of hearts, I believed that my father was right—that the most important thing was to manifest the gifts that were granted us.

Then one day the door opened and a eunuch told me to follow him. The light was so blinding after endless days of darkness that it hurt my eyes. I was grateful for the eunuch's strong hand on my arm, catching me when I stumbled in the bright light.

I wanted to ask the eunuch why I had been let out, but I knew it would not be proper to ask such a question. "What am I supposed to do now?" I asked instead.

"Exactly what you were doing before. Return to your dormitory, to your oda, and to your work in the gardens," he said. Then he added some advice: "And stay out of trouble."

After being in prison, I felt such gratitude to be returning to the pavilions and fountains of the gardens, and the cheerful girls and the eunuchs of the harem. I was happy just being outdoors in the sun again, feeling the mild breeze on my skin. It was like being returned to life.

The first thing I did was to check on my tulips. They were limp and neglected. I immediately began watering, feeding, and talking to them. I told them that I was back to nurture them, and soon they responded.

When I went to check up on my remaining drawings, I found nothing. Nothing! Could I have put them elsewhere and not remember where? I looked under other crevices and planks, everywhere, again and again. But they were gone, nowhere to be found.

Who could have taken them? Was it someone who had accidentally found them and destroyed them but didn't know they were mine? Someone who wanted to protect me—like the Mistress of the Flowers? Or someone who wanted to bring me harm?

20 *Princess Fatma*

That afternoon, I was summoned by Princess Fatma. The first thought that occurred to me was that something had happened to Lena.

Princess Fatma's pavilion was different from any other part of the harem. It was in chaos—there were toys, pillows, books, and things scattered everywhere. The Princess looked disheveled, not as elegant and collected as she had been the other times I'd seen her.

"Semiramis! I'm running out of patience. You've made another mess," the Princess called out. "Where are you?"

Lena came in, and when she saw me, she ran to me and threw her arms around my legs. I was relieved to see that nothing was wrong with her. She looked healthy and well-groomed. Obviously the Princess took good care of her.

The Princess then turned to me. "You're here. Finally. I have wanted to talk to you. First, tell me this. Do you know this child?"

"Yes, my lady, we were brought to İstanbul on the same ship," I said, a bit reluctantly since I was not sure of her intentions. I did not want the Princess to be jealous of our connection.

She asked me to tell her where I came from, how I landed here, and anything I knew of the child's past. I told her what little I knew. "Her real name is Lena."

"Once she was Lena," the Princess said forcefully. "Now she is *Semiramis*. Once she was a peasant girl; now she must learn to behave like a Princess, because she is my doll. I want her to be perfect in all things."

"Yes, of course, my lady," I replied.

"What oda do you belong to?" she asked me.

"I work in the gardens."

She smiled meaningfully. "Ah, yes, I'm told that you grow tulips and that you have other 'talents.'"

"I'm not sure I understand." I did not know what she meant, but I was nervous.

"I think you are pretending to know less than you do. Apparently, you don't hesitate to copy the work of the Almighty," she said with a slight smile.

I felt myself turning red. "I . . . I'm not sure I know what you are suggesting, my lady," I stammered.

"My brother, Prince Mejnun, told me that he has seen you go to the garden and paint pictures of flowers."

So it was he! It was the Prince who had left the note attached to my drawings! He had to be the one to have stolen my paintings! But why? Did he intend for me to get into more trouble, so that I would be punished more? Yet Belkıs had told me he did not have a mean bone in his body, and I believed her. I prayed it was true, since I didn't cherish the thought of losing my head, as he had once threatened. But why was his sister being nice to me now?

"He thought the pictures were beautiful," the Princess continued. "He had not seen paintings like that before—of real things. He thinks I should learn from you. I've seen some of your paintings and drawings and appreciate the sensitivity of your expression. That's why I arranged for you to be released."

"It was you? Oh, Princess, I'm so grateful."

"You see, I like drawing and calligraphy myself," she continued. "I don't think I have much talent, though. That's why I threw my calligraphy out—it was on the other side of the papers on which you made your drawings."

So it was her discarded paper that I had been drawing on? Everything seemed to be coming full circle.

"I would like to ask you to teach me and Semiramis how to draw the way you do. For me, it's just an entertainment. But Semiramis needs a good education."

"I'm surprised, Princess, that you are not against making images of living things. The Chief Housekeeper warned me about it and told me to forget about painting because the Prophet declared that it was forbidden to imitate God."

"I don't think that's what the Prophet meant," she said firmly. "We are not imitating God. We are channeling. Channeling his energy into a form of beauty. That's why we exist—to be the instruments of God. God is beauty. And it's our duty to express that."

The Princess impressed me with her willfulness. I thought to myself that this was something we had in common. But hers was forceful and confident, while mine was quieter. What she had said also reminded me of my beloved father.

Life is strange. The Princess gave me a little room where I could draw and practice calligraphy. Every day I worked with her and Lena. I had lots of paper and paints, and I was suddenly doing things I loved.

One day the Princess showed me some pictures of *gavours*, Europeans dressed in our clothes. "The French ambassador, Monsieur Villeneuve, sent them as a wedding present."

"I didn't expect their people to be dressed just like us," I commented.

"Villeneuve said they imitate the way the Turks dress. They decorate their houses to look like ours. They even call these fads *turqueries*."

"What does that mean?"

"It means things Turkish."

So began my relationship with Princess Fatma. I think she told me things she didn't tell others. She said I understood her. I was afraid that other girls would become jealous of our relationship and would try to harm me, because life in the harem could be so competitive. Princess Fatma's attentions might make me a target. But what could I do?

"I was married to a Vizier when I was five years old, and we had a fabulous wedding," the Princess told me. "My husband was not at the wedding. I had a gorgeous gown of swan feathers—I still remember it. My hair was divided into a thousand and one ringlets through which strings of pearls were threaded. My husband sent lots of presents to celebrate the occasion."

"But you never met him?" I asked.

"No. The Pasha was killed in the war in Petervardin and left me a widow when I was seven."

"I'm so sorry."

"Actually, the marriage was nothing more than a contract," she said, almost indifferently.

"And your new marriage?" I dared to ask.

"The Grand Vizier is a clever man and my father's best friend. He is cultured. He has built many schools and inspires our people with the joy of learning. He established the empire's first printing press and mint. We have many writers now who are reproducing manuscripts and books. It is because of him that the women read and write poetry. Before him, this was also forbidden. He is a good man, and I am honored."

I could see that the age difference didn't matter to the Princess. Obviously, she herself was more interested in knowledge.

21 *Anticipation*

Princess Fatma's wedding was planned for April, to coincide with the Tulip Festival. It would last two days and two nights during the full moon. It was to be more lavish and more spectacular than any other festival that had ever taken place in İstanbul. That was saying a lot, because the Padishah was known for the lavishness of his festivals. The festivities would also celebrate the completion of the Sadabad Palace and would celebrate the Padishah's youngest sons now that they were becoming men.

Everyone in the city was invited to celebrate. Women would be permitted to uncover their faces and speak in public. Even the women in the Sultan's harem would be allowed to take part in the festivities. Since I had arrived, I had never been outside the palace, so it was exciting to think of being able to see İstanbul from beyond the harem walls.

Master Hyacinth was in charge of organizing the festivities. He seemed to be everywhere at once. We saw him bustling through the harem more often now, instructing and consulting with various department heads about every detail of the festivities.

"This kind of festival happens once in a lifetime! You'll never see anything like this again. The Padishah wants it to be the most wonderful day ever. People will be coming from all over the empire and the whole city will celebrate, so we must play up to his expectations," I overheard him say.

We all had to work twice as hard to make everything ready. The Topkapı gardens and terraces were groomed and cleaned. Famous dancers were brought in to teach the harem dancers the latest dances. The chefs from the French Embassy trained fifteen hundred cooks to prepare the wedding feast. Sadabad Palace was almost complete, and I heard some of the eunuchs describe it as a cross between the French palace of Versailles and the *Taj Mahal*. One of the other garden novices said that forty orange trees had arrived as a gift from France, and they had been placed in huge pots leading from the edge of the water to the main entrance of the Sadabad.

Twelve hundred tulip bulbs arrived from Holland, the northern land where tulip cultivation was an art, to go with all those tulips already being grown in İstanbul. I helped the Mistress of the Flowers and another acemi open package after package of bulbs. Each package had something in another language and even in another alphabet written on it. One of the eunuchs told me the writing was Latin. I could see that our silent Mistress knew all these bulbs, and I wished that she could talk and tell us their names.

I was thrilled when the *tellâls* announced to the city that prizes would be offered for the best and the most unusual tulips. The Padishah himself had offered a grand prize of one hundred *akças* of gold for a pure black tulip. This had never been seen anywhere, even in Holland, although I had heard that tulip growers had been attempting to produce a black tulip both here in İstanbul and in Holland. I knew that the closest had been of a nut-brown color, but no one had succeeded in producing a black tulip. Cengiz and I had found dark-colored tulips in the hills near our home and had been working to produce even darker flowers when I left. Those were the tulip bulbs that I had brought with me. When the tulips flowered, I would know if we had succeeded.

My bulbs were growing well and were blended in with the rest of the palace bulbs. Since I had my own beds, none of the other gardeners suspected that I had planted anything other than the bulbs I had been given by the Mistress of the Flowers. Maybe the Mistress suspected what I was doing, but in her own curious way, she continued to let me be. I didn't understand this, but I was grateful to her. As I worked, I often wondered how she had come to be the Mistress of the Flowers. But of course, there was no way to ask her. As I tended the beds, I sensed every vein of the tulips and meditated on the hidden treasures of their chalices. I talked to them every day and prayed that they would help me fulfill my dream of reuniting my family by my finding favor with the Padishah. But I never, ever said aloud what my dream was. I thought that if I did, it too would disappear. I had lost so much already, and I didn't dare risk losing this last dream.

The seamstresses were working day and night to create ceremonial costumes for the Princess and other court women. Everyone else in the harem was busy with her own costume, too. I still did not possess any fine clothes of my own and I did not know how to sew. Too embarrassed to ask the other girls to loan me anything, as they had once before, I remained silent. Without Belkıs there to confide in, I said nothing to anyone. Some bundle ladies visited the harem, bringing lovely fabrics from Damascus. They had silks and brocades, laces and golden thread. How could I possibly afford them? Since I was still an acemi and my training was not complete, I was not yet able to earn slipper money, like the more advanced girls did. I had no worldly goods except my secret tulips and the gold coin that the poet at Madam Siranush's market had given me. I wondered if it was he who had recommended me to Master Hyacinth in the first place. But as much as I longed for new clothes to wear for the Tulip Festival, I didn't want to spend that coin.

It meant something other than money to me. It was a good luck charm, as the tin soldier was, and the reminder of the kindness of a stranger.

I held the coin up. "Thank you for being kind to me, and for letting me and my tulip bulbs find a place in a garden here in İstanbul," I whispered. I didn't say how much I wished to be able to take part in the festivities, because I didn't want to seem greedy.

I couldn't burden the Princess with my problems when she was so busy with the preparations for her wedding. Besides, I was there to help her, not the other way around. As she chattered on about everything that was being done for her wedding, I quietly continued our lessons, helping Lena hold the charcoal pencil correctly, showing the Princess how to blend colors with subtlety. As we worked, we were constantly interrupted by someone or other coming to discuss some new detail of the wedding with the Princess. Then the day came when the Princess was so busy that she announced that we should temporarily stop our drawing lessons. "I cannot concentrate right now on drawing and painting. But we will resume again after I am married and have moved to the palace that İbrahim Pasha is building for me. You and I and Semiramis will then continue our lessons there," she said. I was delighted to hear this, of course, but it did not solve my immediate problem.

After that, I devoted all to my tulips. I meditated on the theories that Cengiz and I had developed, that the tulip borrows its colors from the elements—from the sun's patient heat and from the makeup of the soil, clear water, juices of the earth, and cool breezes. Those tulips that I expected to be darkest were those most exposed to the sun.

I had heard that İbrahim Pasha liked a tulip called the "Blue Pearl" and that he had offered a reward to anyone who would be able to grow one. I suspected that crossing a "Vagrant Smoke" tulip with one called "Silver Flame" could yield such a color. If there had been more time, I knew I could have produced one. It would have been a perfect wedding present for the Princess. But I had my hopes pinned on another color—the color preferred by the Sultan. I knew it would take a miracle to produce it, and I prayed for that miracle. But who was I to ask, when the most illustrious tulipists had been unsuccessful?

Now that all the tulips were about to bloom, I hardly slept. The first thing every morning, I hurried to my garden bed. As the day before the festivities arrived, all of my care and attention paid off. Along with the hundreds of other tulips I had been tending, my own three tulips were just showing signs of opening. Using branches artfully arranged in the bed, I carefully shielded them so that no one else would see them.

22 *The Miracle*

I awoke on the day of the Tulip Festival with a heavy heart, knowing that I would not be able to attend the festivities. I knew it would be seen as disrespectful if I appeared in my everyday clothes, which were worn and stained from my work in the gardens. Would it always be that what I wanted most was beyond my grasp?

When I opened my closet to dress for my work in the garden, I gasped. Inside was an exquisite blue velvet kaftan, embroidered with silver thread. It looked as if it were meant for someone in the royal family, not for a lowly harem apprentice like me. What was it doing in my closet? Who had the right to go in there? I was afraid one of the other girls might have stolen it and put it there to get me into trouble. But there was a note attached to it. "Do not ask who sends you this gift.

Enjoy the blessings of your fate."

I dressed quickly in the beautiful blue kaftan and hurried outside to the garden. I came upon a great commotion in the courtyard. Everyone was making a fuss over hundreds of live turtles that had just been delivered. I watched for a few minutes as the housekeeping staff grabbed turtle after turtle and started putting candles on the turtles' backs. I wouldn't understand why until later that evening.

I continued to the garden, and what I saw made me the happiest girl on earth. The day had started with miracles, and I prayed to Allah that it would continue that way.

The gardens and fields along the waterfront were filled with jugglers, tightrope walkers, acrobats, fire eaters, dancing bears, dwarfs, wrestlers, and poets. Silver wax trees covered with mirrors, flowers, and jewels were everywhere. I had never imagined such a scene.

That afternoon, the Padishah sat in a pavilion near the waterfront on a golden dais, giving out prizes. It was the moment of the tulip competition, and I stood among the other tulipists in my beautiful kaftan, waiting for my turn to unveil my prize. I held my precious tulip, covered with a scarf, close to me. Suddenly Master Hyacinth gave a signal and cannons exploded. I stood with nervous anticipation as the tulipists one by one proudly displayed their tulips. They were so beautiful—each one of them! There were colors that I had not seen before. Some were of a deep, solid color, with beautifully rounded petals. Others were multicolored with contrasting colors running through them. Some even had petals that were almost frilly. Then it was my turn. Nervously I unveiled my tulip, which was much darker than any other that had been presented, and gasps rose all around me. Proudly, I offered the black tulip to the Padishah, who smiled with delight. At the clap of the Padishah's hands, Master Hyacinth stepped forward and with a flourish presented me with a bag of coins.

"Congratulations, young miss," he said quietly to me. "The poet was right about you." Before I could say anything, he turned back to attend to the Padishah.

Clutching the bag, I thought about my poor mother and wished I could present this to her and my brother Cengiz. Was it not Cengiz's work also that produced the black tulip? Then I noticed the Mistress of the Flowers watching me. I turned to her, worried that she might think I was taking a prize for tulips that weren't mine, but she smiled and nodded—and I knew she understood everything. But before I could make my way over to her, she slipped away, melting beyond the crowd in her silent and mysterious way. I turned back to the other tulipists, all of whom were men. They were busily talking to one another and gesturing at my tulip and their own tulips, but no one approached me, even to congratulate me. Was it because they were jealous, or because they did not know how to talk to a girl, especially one from the Sultan's harem?

Night fell as if we all were in a dream. The turtles were released, becoming magic lights moving slowly, mysteriously through the dark. A fleet of decorated galleys lit with torches cruised along the coast. Constellations of the most extraordinary fireworks exploded on the seven hills of the city, announcing that the wedding had taken place. That night the harem women were free to show off their beauty. Groups of them moved freely about, escorted only by the ever-present eunuchs. People whispered that at the wedding, İbrahim Pasha had recited love verses to his young bride that expressed his poetic and genuinely deep feelings for her. In turn, she had sung love songs to him. Music and poetry and beauty and light filled the air and the world seemed perfect. Leaving the magic night, I returned to the dormitory, where I fell asleep instantly and slept a deep, dreamless sleep.

The next day, there were sports competitions near where the tulip competition had taken place. I watched Prince Mejnun throwing a javelin. He was graceful and fast. I knew, because I had often watched Cengiz with the javelin.

Afterward, he noticed me. "So we meet again—but this time you don't have to hide. I will not cut off your head," he said, teasing me.

"Yes, sir," I replied with my eyes down, feeling shy.

"Everyone is talking about your black tulip, which has given our Padishah the greatest pleasure. But I think that you are an artist as well as a prize-winning tulipist. I was wondering if you would like to meet the two greatest artists of our time."

"I don't believe I deserve the honor, sir."

"And I believe that is for them to decide. Please follow me," he said, indicating a walkway that led toward the waterfront.

Suddenly, there in front of us was the poet from the slave market, the one who had given me the gold coin. Once again, our paths had crossed! He was reciting one of the poet Nedim's more famous poems.

Come SONG!
Let's grant joy to this heart of ours
    that flutters in distress:
Let's go to the pleasure gardens,

come, my sauntering cypress . . .
Look, at the dock, a six-oared boat
is waiting in readiness—
Let's go to the pleasure gardens,
come, my sauntering cypress . . .

His eyes rested on me with recognition. "I see that her kısmet has brought my sauntering cypress to the pleasure gardens," he said, bowing deeply in front of me. "And that the tulip bulbs you were so generous with at the slave market last year carry magic in them." Then he saluted the Prince, as people around us began to applaud his recitation. Suddenly, he disappeared into the crowd, reciting other verses as he did.

Prince Mejnun turned to me. "You know, they say that your kısmet is written on your forehead when you are born—and that it is your map through life. You cannot change it and you cannot steal another's kısmet."

I pondered what the poet had said about my kısmet. Had my destiny led me here? "Who was that man?" I asked Prince Mejnun.

"The Nightingale is what we call him, but his real name is Nedim. He is the greatest poet of our time and is one of the artists I wanted you to meet. He is the real spirit of our city, and he sings the beauty of our city like no other. He wanders among the rich and the poor alike and captures their imagination."

I couldn't contain my excitement. It had been Nedim himself, the renowned poet, who had given me the special coin that day at the market—who had recommended me to Master Hyacinth. And here I was, having gained favor with the Padishah, the Princess, and handsome Prince Mejnun.

"That was really Nedim?" I was trying to make sense of it all and thinking about destiny.

"Yes. Do you know his poetry?" The Prince recited a fragment of one of Nedim's poems in a singsong voice. "'Let us all laugh and play. Let us fully enjoy the world's delights.'" When he stopped, he said to me, "Don't worry. Laugh. Be happy. We are put on this planet to enjoy what life has to offer. I agree with my father that we should celebrate instead of warring with other people. We should cultivate what the muses have given us. We must rejoice. Dance . . . sing . . . recite poetry. Let us get drunk with life. Let us cultivate nature . . . create the most beautiful gardens, the most beautiful houses, palaces, mosques . . . Let us create beauty!"

I listened in disbelief as the Prince continued. "I know you feel this, too, because I have seen what you have done. I've seen your beautiful black tulip and your paintings. You have beauty inside you."

I was not used to praise, or even notice, and I didn't know what to say. I looked down, wondering why the Prince was favoring me so.

Then the Prince led me to an old mill that had been converted into an enormous studio. Inside, dozens of artists were hunched over low tables, drawing scenes from the festival even as it was taking place. These had to be the miniaturists my father had told me about. Among them was a heathen, the Prince told me, an artist from Holland, the kingdom where they were mad about tulips. He was called Vanmour. I was intrigued by his style and how he made everything look so real. Every person in his paintings looked different. I stopped, struck by a picture he was painting of our Padishah. I had never seen such a portrait of a real person before and the resemblance was so real that it shocked me.

Next we went into a part of the studio where an older man sat on the floor before a low table. He was surrounded by some of the most beautiful miniatures I had ever seen. Even though they were unfinished, I could see that they portrayed a sequence of events occurring at the festival, real events—like those my father had set off to war to paint. The icons of Christian saints that Father painted were imaginary, but these were pictures of what was really happening right here and now. I was enchanted.

The man stood up when he saw the Prince and greeted him with warmth. I stood slightly behind the Prince, feeling a bit shy.

"This is the girl," Prince Mejnun said to the painter. To me he said, "This is Master Levni, the greatest Ottoman artist, the recorder of our visual history."

Master Levni turned and pulled something out of one of the many drawers. It was my tulip paintings.

So it obviously had been Prince Mejnun who had taken them to him.

"These are very good," Levni said, "as if you were taught by someone very skilled. Where did you learn to paint like this, young maiden?"

"From my father," I told him reluctantly. "He . . . he was the best-known artist in Georgia. He taught my brother and me to draw and paint."

"And he is still there?" Master Levni asked.

"No," I said. "At least, he wasn't when I left. But I pray that he has returned by now. My mother . . ." I stopped, realizing that I was saying more than I should. Prince Mejnun and Master Levni were watching me intently.

Master Levni said, "I employ the most gifted artisans of the empire, some of whom were prisoners of war, but I do not know of your father." He paused and coughed before continuing. "The guilds don't allow women, but with the Prince's permission, I'll make an exception and invite you into my guild. An artist like you is valuable. You shall work with me."

"Thank you, sir. But what about my work with

Princess Fatma? And my job in the gardens?" I looked at the Prince.

"If Master Levni, the greatest artist in the empire, desires it, it shall be. I will arrange it," he said firmly.

As I lay in bed that night, I ran through the recent events in my mind once again. So many magical things had happened in the course of just two days. Only a short while ago, I was alone in a dark, musty prison cell, wishing I was dead. But yesterday and today, I magically had been able to walk in freedom among the people of the entire city. I had seen amazing events and celebrated with all of İstanbul. And as if that weren't enough, I had won the tulip contest, I had walked with the Prince, and I had met the most glorious artists of my time.

All this seemed like a dream, a fantastic dream. I prayed to Allah to protect me from the evil eye of those who might be jealous of me. I touched my left shoulder to find the charm that protected me, and clutching it, I fell asleep. That night, I slept better than any other night since I had arrived in İstanbul.

23 *Heart's Desire*

Two days later, the Chief Housekeeper told me that I was to report to Master Levni's guild instead of going to the gardens. One of the eunuchs would escort me there.

"Be sure to cover yourself when you leave the harem. And also in the guild!" From the way she spoke, I didn't think she approved of my new placement, but I guessed that Prince Mejnun had insisted, possibly over the objections of many.

Master Levni's guild was decorating a new library the Padishah was building near the Cannon Gate—the Sultan Ahmet Library. When I entered it that first day, I inhaled deeply the scent of the paints that were being used. I wondered what Father would think of my being assigned to work under Master Levni. It felt strange but a privilege to be the only girl in the guild, working behind lattices so that none of the guild members could see me. My identity was kept a secret, and I was allowed to talk to no one except the master himself. He gave me instruction in miniature painting and commented on my work. He also allowed me to see the work of the other artists in the guild.

In the evenings, I was escorted back to the harem and was once again surrounded by women. It seemed a strange life. Why did women and men live so separately here? Was one better than the other? Men had the freedom to go wherever they wished, which I could see was a great advantage. And the women and children were safe and well provided for, and never lacked for company, as I know my mother had. But I thought it would be best if the men, women, children—people of all ages—all lived together, as they did in my village.

One morning, as a eunuch accompanied me to the library, we crossed the courtyard of roses. From one of the rooms that gave onto the courtyard came a great deal of noise and commotion, and I could hear the voices of men from inside.

"What are they doing?" I asked the eunuch.

"They are creating a new room and painting murals on the walls. The Padishah wants to build a room representing every fruit. It will be called the Fruit Room," he said.

As we passed close to a window, I heard a voice among the painters that made me stop. I stopped and pretended to adjust my slippers as I listened carefully to the words, the intonation, and the foreign accent. It was unmistakably his voice. But how could that be? It was impossible. It had to be a voice that only sounded like his, which confused me and made me sad and homesick. Tears rolled down my cheeks. Suddenly, I was no longer Leyla at Topkapı Palace in İstanbul, but Laleena at home in Georgia. My parents, my brothers—they all came alive in my mind. I wanted to stay and listen to the voice all day long, but the eunuch was impatient to keep moving, so he hurried us away.

I couldn't get that voice out of my mind as I worked in the library. I began to believe that the voice really did belong to my father. What if his kısmet—his destiny—had also led him here to the court of the Padishah? Unable to resist any longer, I wrote a brief note in Georgian script, folded it, and put my father's name on it. I wrote that he should leave a response under the broken rock under the yellow rosebush in the courtyard. As I returned to the harem at the end of the day, I found a way to slip the note under the door of the Fruit Room without the eunuch noticing.

The next day I found a response. My heart soared to see that familiar handwriting! My hands trembling, I opened the note. It wasn't signed but it was indeed from my father! The message was short—I guessed that he feared it would be dangerous for both of us if he was seen writing it. He explained that he had been taken as a prisoner of war, had been brought here to

İstanbul, and was now employed in an artists' guild, but a different one from Master Levni's.

I wanted so badly to see him, but it was impossible. I was always accompanied by a eunuch and not allowed to leave the library until the end of the day. I tried to linger near the courtyard of roses on the way to the library, but our hours didn't coincide, and we both knew it would be foolish and dangerous to arrange a secret meeting. Instead, we continued leaving letters in the garden. I wrote to him about how things had been with my mother and brothers before I left. Then I told him about my own mixed fortunes that had made me a slave but that had also brought me to the Padishah's harem, where I had accomplished so much. I wrote to him about my tulips and about being part of Master Levni's guild. He was proud of me, he wrote back. The ink had run from his tears.

I was putting into calligraphy a beautiful poem Prince Mejnun had written on a dry leaf. It was to go on the wall of Sultan Ahmet's library, along with some of the Padishah's own poetry, as he himself was a master poet. Calligraphy, like music, I had learned, reveals the emotions of the moment. I was very moved by the Prince's poem. And at the same time, my emotions were so focused on wanting to see my father that I, in turn, expressed my emotions through the characters I was creating. It was the most beautiful rendering I had ever created.

When Prince Mejnun came to visit our guild, he read the lines of his poem as I had written them. He was clearly moved by the beautiful rendering I had done. "Thank you," he said.

I blushed and turned away my head, saying nothing. I think he felt embarrassed himself. After a moment, he reached for his pocket and pulled out a small sack of coins. He leaned over to give it to me.

I shook my head. "No, Prince Mejnun, I cannot accept that. You have already been very kind to me, for which I am grateful. But I'm not interested in gold. That is not my heart's desire."

"What then is your heart's desire, Leyla?"

I didn't know how to begin. What could I say? But I had to say something, even to risk everything I had gained. I took a deep breath. "Once upon a time, there was a master painter in the Caucasus," I began. "He had a sweet wife and four children. They lived in happiness and bliss, until the wretched wars began. Then the master went to war as an artist—and he never returned. His family was distraught. They had barely enough to eat."

The Prince was listening attentively. I could see that he was captivated but also uncertain why I was telling him such a story.

"So the master's daughter sold herself to the slave traders and her destiny brought her to İstanbul, to the Padishah's Palace of Topkapı. There, with the help of kısmet and some kindness from a Prince, a Princess, and a poet, she found herself doing the two things she loved most in the world: growing tulips and painting. In her new life, she had found some inner happiness, some deep expression of her spirit."

"But why are you telling me this story?" asked the Prince.

I smiled at him but continued my story. "Then one day she heard a familiar voice in the palace. It was a voice she knew well, a voice she had known since she was born," I continued. "It was her father's voice. His kısmet had also brought him to the Padishah's palace."

"You mean—" Prince Mejnun looked at me with disbelief.

"Yes, sir, my father is *here*. He was brought here as a prisoner of war and is employed at this very moment painting the Fruit Room."

Prince Mejnun asked me more questions. He put away his gold, but he told me before he left that he would do his best to help my father and me. He didn't know how, and he said he couldn't promise anything because the decision would not be up to him, but he would try.

A week passed, during which my father's voice disappeared. I no longer received messages from him either, and those I left for him were not picked up. I was worried sick. What had they done to him? Would I be able to find him again? Had he been expelled? Had Prince Mejnun betrayed me after all?

I buried myself in my work again. One afternoon, Master Levni arrived, asking to look at my most recent botanical drawings. He was accompanied by another man, so I kept my eyes down modestly. But then something made me look up. My heart stopped, then started again. I jumped up and ran into my father's arms. He held me and kissed me and neither of us spoke at first, our tears rolling down our cheeks. "Praise be to Allah, for here you are," he finally said. "I have missed you so much."

Master Levni left us alone. We sat together just looking at each other, still unable to talk. My father looked older, more worn, and he seemed to walk with a limp. But his deep brown eyes were warm and filled with love, and I was happier than I had ever been.

Finally, Father broke the silence. "Laleena, my dearest, I have been granted amnesty."

"What does it mean, Father?"

"It means that I am free and can return to Georgia," he said. "I asked for you to come with me, but it is not possible." New tears sprang to his eyes. "Oh, my dear daughter! How can this be?"

It was another moment of sadness mixed with joy. Just as we had reunited, we had to part again.

"But I am so happy for you, Father. And for Mother, and Cengiz, and the twins—oh, it will be so good for you all to be together again. You will be able to return to your old lives!"

"Returning to things is never as you left them. Once you were Laleena, a sweet Georgian maiden, and look at you now. Now you are Leyla. You still have the essence of that sweet girl, but I can see that you are an independent, self-assured young lady now. I can see that you have manifested many of the gifts that swirl inside you. You have achieved a great sense of freedom, freedom within yourself, which is the greatest freedom of all. Even in slavery, our spirits can sustain us."

He was saying things that I had felt inside when I was at work painting here in the guild but did not know quite how to put into words.

"I'm happy to be returning home after such a long absence, to be able to see your lovely mother again and your brothers," he continued. "But you cannot imagine the pain I feel having to leave you behind."

"Oh yes, I can, Father," I cried. "I feel it, too."

"But here is one thing for us to hold on to. The Padishah has been pleased with my craft. He has asked me to return, if I so choose, with my family—but as a free man. He has said he has many other projects for me."

My face lit up. "You would, all of you, come here to İstanbul, then?"

"I'm not sure yet, my daughter. I will know when I return home. We must think of the rest of the family. They might be content with their lives now. They may like the security of living in their homeland. When people are content, it is not easy to stir them to change. I will have to see."

Prince Mejnun had kindly granted us an afternoon together. I could not show Father my tulip bed inside the harem, but he saw the tulips I had painted. I could see that he was proud of my work. I gave him several of the paintings to take back as gifts to the family and most of the gold the Sultan had given me for producing the black tulip. I also returned to my tulip bed and dug up some tulip bulbs.

"These are for Cengiz. They are the bounty from the bulbs I borrowed before I left home. I also have some instructions for him about cultivating them." I didn't tell him that one of those bulbs belonged to the black tulip. I wanted it to be a surprise. Cengiz would have to discover it himself.

I gave my father the blue velvet kaftan embroidered with silver thread. My beautiful mother deserved to look like a Sultana. Then we said a tearful good-bye.

I had found and lost my father again. But I felt grateful that I had been reunited with him, even for such a short time. There was both peace and hope in my mind. Since it had happened once, it could happen again. I also realized that my work at the guild and in my tulip garden made me happy. I now had friends in Belkıs, little Semiramis, Princess Fatma, Master Levni, and Prince Mejnun. I felt a special warmth for the Prince because of all he had done for me.

I had made a new life for myself, one that I had grown into through pain, hard work, kindness, and luck. Maybe having talent was that combination of things. I was far from my homeland, but this was where I belonged for now.

The rest was up to kısmet.

Then and Now ♦ *A Girl's Life*

T U R K E Y

The Hall of the Sultan is located inside the harem.

The word *harem* means "protected" or "forbidden." When Leyla passed through the Gate of Felicity, or Great Happiness, into the Topkapı Palace harem, she entered a world both protected and forbidden. It was a world of splendor and of servitude—a world ruled by the wishes of one man, the *Sultan*, or emperor.

By the early 1700s, when Leyla's story takes place, Turkey was part of a vast empire that had been ruled by Ottoman sultans for nearly 400 years. At its height, the Ottoman Empire stretched across three continents, including eastern Europe, northern Africa, parts of the Middle East, and southern Russia. At the center of this empire, in the city of İstanbul, the domes and turrets of Topkapı Palace shone like jewels. More a small city than a palace, Topkapı was a complex of royal chambers,

The Topkapı Palace harem was a special world of women.

courtyards, government headquarters, mosques, workshops, kitchens, and baths. In the middle of this bustling metropolis was a city within a city—a place where women, children, and a few special servants lived and worked behind high walls—the harem.

Like Leyla, most girls came to the harem as slaves, kidnapped or captured in war, or sold by their desperately poor families. Traders traveled to distant corners of the empire, such as Leyla's home in the Caucasus Mountains, in search of girls for the Sultan's harem. To be chosen for the harem was considered a privilege and assured a good life for a girl. In the harem, each girl was given a Turkish name, began instruction in Turkish and the customs of the palace, and converted to Islam. As an *odalisque*, or personal servant, a girl learned to

A slave market in İstanbul

read and write, play musical instruments, sing, and dance. If, like Leyla, she had a special talent, she was assigned to train under the watchful eye of the Mistress of the Robes, the Mistress of the Flowers, or another department head. Above all, as she became part of this close community of women, the girl learned to respect the strict rules of the harem.

Every aspect of a girl's life in the harem—even the girl's clothing—depended on her place in the harem's hierarchy. Leyla wore loose, ankle-length pants, or *şalvar*, made of silk and an embroidered, robe-like *kaftan*. Some women added gowns or jackets, too. Scarves were sometimes embroidered with jewels. Shoes were pointed leather slippers, embroidered

High shoes were worn in Turkish baths by both high-ranking ladies and their servants.

A woman's silk kaftan from 18th-century Turkey

with gold cord and pearls for those of high rank. The most important and powerful women in the harem were the Sultan's mother, or *Valide Sultana*, and the Sultan's favorite wives. They wore fur robes and the best jewels, such as diamond belts and headdresses, ruby earrings, and emerald necklaces. Girls like Leyla adorned themselves by weaving golden threads, pearls, and flowers into their hair.

On rare trips outside the harem, even a high-ranking woman dressed plainly and wore a veil to cover her face. No men, other than the Sultan, his sons, and special male servants called *eunuchs*, were allowed in the harem, and no men except one's closest

Women wore veils and covered themselves when they went outside to shield themselves from the eyes of strangers.

Turkey is known for extraordinary architecture and beautiful geometric tilework, such as this tiled panel in the Topkapı Palace harem.

relatives ever saw a woman's face. Most Islamic women followed the tradition of covering themselves—a tradition that many continue today.

Beyond the walls of the harem, Turkish peasant and middle-class girls also lived in relative seclusion in the *haremlik*, or women's quarters. They, too, covered themselves when outside. A girl's marriage was arranged by her family, usually to a man she had never met, and few girls outside the imperial harem learned to read or write.

Although traditions like the harem and the "passing of the veil" from mother to daughter remained strong in Leyla's time, changes were seeping into the Ottoman Empire. The reign of Sultan Ahmet III, known as "the Tulip Era," was a time of relative peace and great interest in the arts. Rare tulips cultivated in Ottoman gardens were sold in Europe at extraordinary prices, inspiring a "tulipomania" that nearly drove one country, the Netherlands, into bankruptcy. Visitors to İstanbul and courtiers who traveled to

Tulips grew wild in the hills near Leyla's home but were later bred for specific colors or characteristics.

Europe brought Western goods and new ideas—ideas that gradually changed the harem way of life.

In 1923, the Republic of Turkey was established. President Kemal Atatürk brought sweeping changes—including forbidding women to wear veils and men to have more than one wife—that created a modern country very different from the Ottoman Empire. Turkish women could vote by 1934. And although most Turkish people today are Muslim, by law families have the right to choose the customs and religious traditions they wish to follow.

Girls and women in Turkey today have a variety of choices. Many girls attend school side by side with boys, listen to pop music, and prepare for careers outside the home; others follow a more traditional Islamic way of life. Turkish women today still enjoy the community of women that has roots in the world of the harem.

Some modern Turkish girls wear scarves, since veils are forbidden, and most follow current fashion.

Glossary

Words other than Turkish words are so identified in the definitions below. Turkish has its own sound system and also borrows from Arabic, Persian, and French, so these pronunciations and some spellings are only approximate.

acemi *(ah-gehm-ee)*—beginners, novices, or interns
aigrette *(ay-greht)*—French word for a jeweled pin used to hold a turban or headscarf closed
akça *(ahk-chah)*—unit of Turkish money
Allahüakbar *(ah-lah-oo-ahk-bahr)*—"God is great."
baklava *(bahk-lah-vah)*—flaky pastry with nuts
Boletus edulis *(boh-leet-us ed-yoo-luhs)*—Latin name for an edible mushroom, such as porcino or cèpe
Bostanjis *(boss-ton-jeez)*—guardians and gardeners of the palace grounds
Bu şehri Stambul ki bimislü bahadır *(boo shehr-ee stun-buhl keeh bee-mihs-leeh bah-huh-dure)*—"This city of İstanbul is matchless, priceless."
caravansaraı *(kah-rah-vahn-sah-rai)*—Persian word for an inn with a courtyard
caïque *(kah-yeek)*—French for a type of rowboat

Cedid Zer-I *(ceh-dihd zehr-eh)*—gold coin bearing the Sultan's name

cennet *(gehn-neht)*—paradise

eunuch *(yoo-nuk)*—English word for a male servant within the harem

feradje *(feh-rah-jeh)*—mantle

gavour *(gah-voor)*—foreigner, non-Muslim

halvah *(hehl-vah)*—dessert made with sesame tahini

halvet *(huhl-veht)*—private outdoor party or outing

hamam *(hah-mahm)*—public bathhouse

harem *(hahr-ehm)*—the women's quarters of a palace

haremlik *(hahr-ehm-lihk)*—the women's quarters in a household

Haseki Sultana *(huh-say-kee suhl-tah-nah)*—the first wife of the Padishah, or Sultan

Haznedar *(hahz-nee-dahr)*—treasurer

hotoz *(hoh-tohz)*—head decoration

hürriyet *(huhr-ree-yet)*—freedom

Hunkar Sofasi *(hoon-kahr soh-fah-see)*—Hall of the Sultan

imam *(ih-mum)*—religious teacher

Janissaries *(jah-nee-sah-reez)*—English word for a

special corps of Ottoman troops or soldiers

kaftan *(kahf-tahn)*—long robe worn by both men and women, usually over loose pants

Kâhya *(kah-yah)*—Chief Housekeeper of the harem

kilim *(kihl-hihm)*—handwoven carpet

kısmet *(kihz-meht)*—fate or destiny

Koran *(kohr-uhn)*—English word for the Muslim holy book

Lailahi Illallah *(lah-ih-lah-ih i-ah-lah)*—"There is no God but God."

medrese *(mehd-reh-seh)*—school, mostly religious

minaret *(mih-nahr-eht)*—tall, narrow tower on a mosque from which daily calls to prayer are sung

Mkhedruli *(mihk-heh-droo-lee)*—Georgian script or alphabet

mosque *(mahsk)*—English word for a Muslim house of worship

müezzin *(muh-eh-zihn)*—one who sings out the call to prayer

namaz *(numb-oz)*—the act of facing the holy city of Mecca and praying

nargileh *(nahr-gihl-eh)*—water pipe

oda *(oh-dah)*—room or department in the harem

odalisque *(od-dah-leesk)*—French word for a personal servant

Ottoman *(aht-teh-muhn)*—English term derived from "Osman," the name of the Turkish dynasty that became a great empire starting in the 1600s

Padishah *(pah-dee-shah)*—ruler or emperor, also called "Sultan"

Pasha *(pah-shah)*—the highest title of a military or civil official

rakı *(rah-kuh)*—an anise-flavored drink

şalvar *(shahl-vahr)*—loose pants worn beneath a kaftan or robe

scimitar *(cee-mee-tahr)*—English word for a sword with a curved blade

selamlık *(seh-lum-look)*—the men's personal quarters within the harem

Sultan *(suhl-tahn)*—Arabic word for ruler, emperor, or king; also called "Padishah"

tandir *(tahn-ihr)*—an oven in the ground

tellâl *(tehl-lull)*—street announcers

tesbih *(tehs-beeh)*—prayer beads

turah *(too-rah)*—the Sultan's signature
turqueries *(tuhr-kehr-eez)*—French word for the fad of using Turkish design in decorating and clothing
ud *(ood)*—stringed instrument resembling a lute
Valide Sultana *(vah-leihd-eh suh-tah-nah)*—mother of the Sultan
Vizier *(veh-zeer)*—high executive officer or minister
yashmak *(yosh-muhk)*—headscarf, also used as a veil

Pronunciation of names and places:
Abkhazia *(ahb-kah-zee-ah)*—a region on the eastern end of the Black Sea
Ahmet *(ah-meht)*—name of a sultan of the Ottoman Empire
Allah *(ah-lah)*—God
Aslan *(ahs-lahn)*—Leyla's father, means "lion"
Atatürk, Kemal *(ah-tah-tuhrk, keh-mahl)*—a Turkish hero who established the Republic of Turkey in the 1920s and became the first president
Batum *(bah-toom)*—city on the Black Sea
Belkıs *(behl-kuss)*—Leyla's friend in Topkapı Palace; means "Queen of Sheba"

Cafer Efendi *(jah-fehr eh-fehn-dee)*—name of the slave trader, means "a small stream"

Cairo *(kai-roh)*—capital city of Egypt

Caucasus *(kaw-kuhs-uhs)*—largely mountainous area to the north and east of the Black Sea

Cengiz *(gehn-gihz)*—Leyla's brother, means "descendant of Genghis Khan"

Circassia *(seer-kuh-see-ah)*—inland region northeast of the Black Sea

Damascus *(dah-mas-kahs)*—capital city of Syria

Fatma *(faht-mah)*—one of the daughters of Sultan Ahmet III

Georgia *(gyohr-gyjah)*—country on the Black Sea

İbrahim Pasha *(ih-brah-hihm pahsh-ah)*—the Grand Vizier of Sultan Ahmet III, during the Tulip Era

İstanbul *(is-stuhn-bul)*—largest city in Turkey and the center of the Ottoman Empire; previously "Constantinople" and "Byzantium"

İzmir *(ihs-meer)*—city in western Turkey, once known as "Smyrna"

Leyla *(lay-lah)*—name meaning "the night and the light that brightens it"

Levni *(lehv-nee)*—one of Turkey's greatest painters
Mejnun *(madge-noon)*—fictional son of Sultan Ahmet III; the hero of the romance *Leyla and Mejnun*; means "madly in love"
Nedim *(neh-dihm)*—great 18th-century Turkish poet
Sadabad *(sah-dah-bahd)*—a colony of palaces built along İstanbul's harbor, later destroyed by fire
Salonica *(sah-lawn-ee-kah)*—city in Greece also known as "Thessaloníki"
Semiramis *(seh-mee-rah-mihs)*—name given to Leyla's friend Lena, also an ancient queen of Babylon
Sümbül Ağa *(sum-buhl ah-ah)*—Master Hyacinth, the chief eunuch in the palace
Taj Mahal *(tahj mah-hahl)*—a palace in India
Topkapı *(toph-kah-puh)*—the Sultan's greatest palace in İstanbul, means "cannon gate"
Trabzon *(trahb-zohn)*—ancient city on the Black Sea once famous for its towers
Vakhtang VI *(vahk-tahng)*—Georgian king, approximately 1703–1724
Versailles *(vehr-sigh)*—name of the palace of French King Louis XIV

Author's Note

When I was in school in İstanbul, my friends and I put on a play called *Lâle Devri*, or "The Tulip Era." We dressed in the gorgeous costumes of the sultanas and tiptoed through a garden of paper tulips reciting lines from Nedim, Turkey's loveliest poet.

I was drawn to history that revealed women's lives. The Tulip Era, as the reign of Sultan Ahmet III was known, was a time in which Turkey opened up to new ideas and women had more freedom. Filled with peace, culture, beauty, poetry, and love of nature, it is my favorite time in Turkish history.

I spent my first eighteen years in Turkey before settling in the U.S. When I returned to İstanbul, I visited the Topkapı Palace harem, which had become a museum. The ladies were long gone, but it was as if the walls whispered stories that needed to be told. It was so real to me that I began to research and write about life in the harem.

I dreamed about a girl who was folding her bedding in a harem dormitory, and she eventually became

Leyla. She is fictional, as are her family and those she meets on her journey—the traders, Lena, Madam Siranush, Belkıs, and others. But many other characters existed as real people, changed a little by me to tell a more personal story.

The Padishah, Ahmet III, and his Vizier, İbrahim Pasha, were indeed opposed to war and created an environment in which poets and painters were celebrated. But they also stopped paying attention to the suffering of their people, which led to an uprising by the Janissaries and put an end to the Tulip Era.

Leyla means "the night and the light that brightens it." My favorite epic is called *Leyla and Mejnun* and is a story of eternal lovers—although it has no resemblance to what might have transpired between Leyla and Prince Mejnun outside the pages of this book.

My fate has taken me to many places in the world. I wanted Leyla to go to a distant place and have a new fate—one that would require intelligence, courage, adaptability, taking risks, and being true to herself. She became a great teacher for me, as I hope she is for you.